"When Dixon's on his game, he's an entertaining writer with an appealingly caustic view of the rich and those hustling to join them."
—Don Napoli, *Reading California Fiction*

"Quite different from the typical pulp novel of the 50s."
—Dave Wilde, Amazon.com

"Dixon's protagonists are men on the outside—rugged, amoral layabouts whose only ambition is to crash the gates of the upper-crust and live the good life."
—Brian Ritt, *Paperback Confidential*

"Dixon's writing is superb on all counts, and he stands out even among noirmasters."
—Kristofer Upjohn, *Noir Journal*

TOO RICH TO DIE

H. Vernor Dixon

Black Gat Books • Eureka California

TOO RICH TO DIE

Published by Black Gat Books
A division of Stark House Press
1315 H Street
Eureka, CA 95501, USA
griffinskye3@sbcglobal.net
www.starkhousepress.com

TOO RICH TO DIE
Originally published by Gold Medal Books, New York, and
copyright © 1953 by Fawcett Publications, Inc.

ISBN: 979-8-88601-127-2

Cover design by Jeff Vorzimmer, ¡caliente!design, Austin, Texas
Text design by Mark Shepard, shepgraphics.com
Proofreading by Bill Kelly

First Stark House Press/Black Gat Edition: December 2024

CHAPTER ONE

I thought of the men who had stared at blank white paper and created great literature, who had painted masterpieces on dull canvas, and who had carved living beauty from cold stone; the men who had designed ocean liners and airplanes and built dams and railroads and factories and highways; the men who had dreamed and worked and sweated and cried out in the night with the agony of creating and building; the men who started with a purpose and worked their way to a definite goal; men so far removed from me that the bile rose in my throat and gagged me.

Bunny had it right. Bunny was saying, "You're nothing but a heel, gold-plated, but still a stinking heel. You've been a spoiled brat all your life and you'll never be anything else. You're less than no good at all because you get in people's lives and ruin them. And you always get away with it because you can afford to buy your way out of anything. But not this time," she cried. "Oh, no. Not this time."

I glanced at her, then looked away to think of the world I was living in, of radar and electronics, jet propulsion and turbines, nuclear fission and The Bomb, of all the vast and sweeping changes taking place and of the men responsible for them. I thought of my place in that world and it was too much to take.

I left the deep chair by the fireplace in Bunny's apartment and staggered to the chrome and glass portable bar against the wall. I was already so drunk I could hardly see, but I needed more. I mixed a highball, slopping some of it on the bar, then looked questioningly at Bunny, the blonde hair tumbling about smooth bare shoulders, her pixie-ish face lacking make-up, shining in the harsh light, the absurd mules on her tiny feet, and the too-feminine negligee held about her trim body by a tight cord. Her eyes slid away from mine to hide the rage burning in their depths.

I sagged back into the chair and sipped the drink. "Better have one."

"I don't need that stuff. I hope to God you drown in it." She took a cork-tipped cigarette from a silver tray on the glass coffee table, got it lit, then leaned back against the fireplace bricks. "Howard, why did you drop by at this hour?"

"I told you, damn it. I want you and Nicky to go back together. This situation is getting ridiculous. So, all right, you and I have been playing around. I set you up in this apartment and we've had fun. But now it's all over and I don't see where I'm responsible for you. Nicky's pretty weak, you know, even as husbands go. He'll take you back. He's still crazy about you. Feed him enough lies and I'm positive he'll take you back."

"Just like that," she sneered. "Oh, no. You don't get off that easy. You're going to pay for this one."

I reminded her, "I gave you a check for fifty thousand last week."

Her cheeks flamed red as she screamed, "That isn't what I mean! You've been getting away with this too often, dozens of times, but not with me. I moved in here with the definite understanding that as soon as I divorced Nicky you would marry me."

I shrugged and said, "Sorry you got the wrong impression. Anyway, it's all over."

"Oh, no, it isn't. You've made an absolute fool of me, so I'm going to make you sweat, too. How did your lovely little Mimi enjoy what I had to tell her about you? She didn't like it much, did she?"

That was it. That was the whole problem. "That," I said, "is why I'm here."

She took a deep drag at the cigarette, then laughed at me. "That's what I thought. Now, I understand, you're on the prowl for the Devereaux girl. Well, I know her, too. And when I get through telling her about you she isn't going to like it, either. You're not going to get anywhere anymore with anyone. Not with me around. You either come back to me or I'll fix your little cart every time. Do you understand?"

I understood well enough. I was understanding so well that an hour before I had dropped into my favorite liquor store in Westwood Village to borrow an automatic pistol which was always under the counter. Sammy Rubin, the proprietor, had not wanted me to have it.

"Geez, Mr. Carleton. The gun's licensed to be kept on the premises, but it don't say nothing about loaning it to anyone. You know I'd like to do you a favor and all that—"

"Sammy, who is your best customer?"

"Well, that's no question. You are. Without your trade," he said, grinning ingratiatingly, "I'd practic'ly be out of business."

"All right. I borrow the gun from you or you lose my trade. There's nothing for you to worry about. I just need it for—well—for a little purpose of my own, and I promise you'll have it back tomorrow."

My butler ordered anywhere from one to two thousand dollars' worth of liquor from Sammy's store per month, an account that Sammy could not afford to lose. He had let me have the gun.

I dropped my hand into my pocket and felt the cold steel of the heavy automatic. The whole idea of the gun was theatrical, but at the moment had seemed basically sound. Bunny, I knew, had a deathly fear of guns of any kind. So I would threaten her with the gun and that would end her intolerable interference in my affairs. My attorneys could not handle that particular situation and evidently money was not enough to smother the fires of her anger. The sight of cold steel should turn the trick, though.

But before I could take the gun from my pocket, she asked, with sudden concern, "Did you park your car in front of the apartment?"

It was hard to dredge even a short memory out of the alcohol I had consumed, but I thought about it and nodded. "Yes."

"If Nicky comes by, he'll recognize it."

"So what?"

"He's been acting very strange lately. He thinks everyone is laughing at him and he's in a murderous rage."

I had to snicker at that. "Nicky? Don't scare me to death."

"Oh, you fool. You never believe anyone has guts enough to do anything."

"Least of all Nicky."

She said tragically, "He loved me, Howard. Still does. He's all mixed up and drinking and going around making threats—"

That reminded me of the gun and my reason for being in the apartment. When I took the gun from my pocket Bunny dropped the cigarette she was holding and all color drained from her face. For a moment I thought she would faint, but she didn't.

I could not hold my hand up, so I propped my elbow on a knee and pointed the gun at her. "Now," I said, "let me explain something to you. You're pressing me too far, my dear. I've paid you off and still you won't let me go. You want revenge."

"Please," she gasped. "Please, put it away. Please, Howard."

"Ugly thing, isn't it? Nothing sporting about it. A pistol has one purpose only, to be used against another human being. Believe me, darling, I won't mind using it on you. I don't like this kind of interfering in my private life. So you're going to drop out of my life as of this moment, or the lovely flesh of that body of yours is going to be badly torn."

She was going out of focus, so I lifted the glass in my other hand and drained it. My sight cleared again for a second or two as her trembling hands grasped a heavy vase she'd taken from the mantel. Her eyes were staring wide, but not quite at me. She seemed to be looking beyond me, toward the other side of the room, her whole body shaking with fear. I felt a draught on the back of my neck, but was too drunk to turn around. I was more interested in her as she cried out, "Please. Oh, my God, no!"

I watched her, more than pleased with the instant success of my little idea, as she swayed back against the cold bricks of the fireplace and threw the vase clumsily. I was too far gone to do any real thinking, but I figured I had won and that made me relax. It also allowed the alcohol to take over and at that moment I either passed out cold or had a temporary blackout of some kind.

I don't know how long I was out, but when I came to I was sprawled down deep in the chair, the glass was lying on the floor at one side and the gun on the floor at the other. Tom-toms were beating in my head, needles were in my eyes, and my mouth tasted like the bottom of a bird cage.

I forced myself to sit up and looked across the room. Bunny was stretched out in a grotesque attitude on the thick, white rug before the fireplace. One arm was bent under her head and her left foot was caught in the crosspiece of a brass andiron. The negligee was practically twisted off her body, exposing her small right breast and the satiny smooth skin of her slender legs. She was not moving or breathing.

It took me a long time to get to my feet. I finally staggered across the room and stood on the edge of the white rug looking down at Bunny. The portion of negligee over her left breast was sticky and red around a small, neat, round hole. Most of the white rug, too, was turning red and blood was seeping in a widening pool into the ashes of the fireplace. I squatted down on my heels, almost falling, and confirmed what was already so obvious. There was nothing anyone could do for Bunny.

I could remember nothing after the time of threatening her with the gun and passing out, and doubted that there was anything to remember. Only one thing could possibly have happened. The gun had been pointed in her general direction. I remembered propping it on my knee. So as I passed out I must have squeezed the trigger and shot her. It was an accident, of course, but she was nevertheless very dead.

I went into the bathroom and was sick, then returned to the living room and swallowed a straight shot of whisky. I thought of using the telephone and stumbled toward it, but changed my mind. Who would I call and what was there to say? I looked around for the gun, but my vision was fuzzy and my eyes kept returning to Bunny. I switched off the lights so I would not have to look at Bunny, poured another heavy slug of whisky, and gulped that down. The full impact of what had happened and how it would seem hit me like a blow and I almost passed out again. The next thing I knew I was frantically staggering around in the dark room trying to find my way out. I had to get away. I had to run.

Fortunately, the door to the apartment hallway was open or I don't think I would ever have found it. I remembered having felt the draught on the back of my neck and wondered if I had left the door open on the way in. I supposed I had. I was so drunk it was impossible to remember much of anything.

I made it outside the apartment house and into the rain. It was raining hard. When it lets go in southern California it doesn't fool around. I ran for the Jaguar, got the powerful engine started, and roared through the dark, river-running streets of Beverly Hills and into Westwood Village and up to Sunset Boulevard. I had a feeling that someone or something was chasing me. Near the Beverly Hills Hotel I swung up into the hills and in a few minutes went through the gates of the old Carleton mansion. Our home had been one of the first built in that area and still dominated all the other estates, in spite of the later influx of movie stars. Sometimes it gave me a chuckle to think of them staring at the Carleton place, faced with the obvious fact that there was more money in oil. But I was not chuckling now.

I went directly to my rooms, poured a stiff shot, and wondered why all the hurry. I was halfway out of my clothes before I realized I wanted to get to the yacht. That was the best place to go. No one would look for me there, at least for a while, and I would have time to think and plan and work things out with my attorneys. I got into some sea-going togs and packed a small bag with spare socks and underwear. I thought of awakening the butler and telling him I would be gone for a few days but decided against that. He was always too overbearingly patient with me when I was drunk.

My eyes closed and I almost fell asleep, but managed to shake myself awake. My mind, by that time, was really going blank. All I could think of was the yacht, but could no longer remember why I wanted to go there.

I took the bag out to the car and headed for an all-night bottle club in Santa Monica. It was a phony plush establishment, but the liquor was good and the half-dressed waitresses were something to watch. After a few drinks I called San Pedro and tried to get through to the yacht, which had a shore line. There was no answer. I tried again later, then remembered that I had given the crew a week's vacation. None of them would be back for another two or three days. I wondered again why I was going to the boat and could not find an answer.

I sat in the club, drinking and thinking about it for probably an hour, until I was so drunk I could hardly get to my feet. I could have remained there, but I had the yacht in mind. I had to get to that boat. I went out to the car and started through the rain toward the shore highway. As soon as I hit the open stretches I jammed down the accelerator. The Jaguar could do better than a hundred and twenty and I had it pressed to the limit. That feeling was on me again, that feeling of floating, of indifference, of not caring what happened. Speed was good. Speed was everything. And somewhere in that speed could be all the solutions I was seeking.

I almost solved them that night.

I was making the turn toward the San Pedro estuary, on the outskirts of the port, when my eyes closed for a fraction of a second. That was long enough at the speed I was traveling.

When I regained consciousness I found myself in the cold gloom of predawn lying on the edge of the rain-wet road. I lay still for a moment, trying to remember. There seemed to be ages missing from time. Then again I saw the curve looming ahead and the lights rushing into it, felt the thunder and the speed of the car and remembered the sickening skid, the blown tire, the automobile starting to spin through space, the rip of the canvas top, and myself hurtling into a black void. I heard the crash and roar of the car turning over on the highway and the sound of a loud splash and then nothing. It came back to me and I was still alive and able to think about it.

I rolled to my side, raised myself cautiously on one hand, and sat up. My clothes were muddy, wet and streaked with oil and road grime. I looked up at the dark sky. The rain had stopped and there was a faint hint of muddy dawn to the east. I got my legs under me and, on all fours, tried to shake my head clear. Too much alcohol. I gave up trying and lurched to my feet.

After falling down and trying again, I stood on uncertain legs, wiped the back of my hand across my mouth, and uncontrollably giggled. Did it again, I thought. The umpteenth time and still alive. To hell with the death wish. It didn't work. You got drunk and drove like crazy and had accidents and nothing could kill you. You made love to other men's wives and fouled their nests and dared them to do something about it and they went to divorce court instead of reaching for a gun. Maybe it was the cautious man who got killed. I had to laugh at that, it seemed so ridiculously true.

I staggered to the edge of the road, blinked in the darkness, and looked down to focus on the scum-oily waters of the San Pedro estuary. At the bottom of the muddy bank was the expensive British convertible. It was almost all under water, but the smashed front wheels, the overlarge headlights, and the typical English radiator projected above the surface. The body of the car could not be seen under the water, but I could imagine its crushed condition. No use going down there. Wreckers could drag it out later. Anyway, it was no great loss. The garage at home was full of cars.

I shrugged and started walking up the road toward San Pedro. I needed a drink. Nothing would be open at that hour, but the yacht was in harbor and the galley would be well stocked. That, I remembered, was where I had been heading when the accident occurred. But why the yacht? Something to do with Bunny. A cruise? Not in that weather. A party on the yacht? I could not remember. I fastened my attention on a vision of the bottle-filled galley.

An occasional automobile passed me on the road, but I was in such a daze it never occurred to me to try thumbing a ride. I left the highway as it entered town and followed the street that ran along the water's edge. My legs were weak and dragging, my head was throbbing, my lips were dry, and my sight was dimming even with the dawn. I stumbled and fell repeatedly. At last I realized, foggily, that I must have been hurt. I needed sanctuary somewhere and what I needed I could buy.

The last time I fell I saw a wharf just ahead and a boat tied up at its side. It was a fishing boat of some kind, like a small purse seiner. There would probably be someone aboard.

I stumbled out the length of the wharf and looked down on the cluttered deck of the boat. My legs gave way and I pitched forward. I landed on the deck with a searing pain in my shoulder, rolled to my back, and closed my eyes.

When I regained consciousness I was lying in a narrow, cramped bunk against the cold plates of a boat's hull. There were seven other bunks in the semi-triangular room, three of them containing sleeping men. A shaded light bulb glowed overhead. There were no ports, so I knew I was in a below-decks forecastle, obviously in the bow.

A giant of a man was leaning back against the opposite bunks, smoking a cigarette and looking down at me. He was one of the most powerful-looking men I had ever seen. He was well over six feet, four inches tall, with ox-yoke shoulders, narrow hips, and long muscles like steel bands in his thick forearms. His yellow-blond hair was cropped close in a crew cut, his skin was leathery, tanned, and wind and sun wrinkles were deep in the corners of his narrowed blue eyes. He was wearing knee boots, dirty suntans, and a filthy gabardine shirt with the officer's tabs still on the shoulders. There was neither sympathy nor pity in the glance he bestowed on me, but rather a cold stare of speculative appraisal.

I swung my feet out of the blankets and sat on the edge of the bunk. I rubbed a hand over my eyes and forehead and held it before my face. It was covered with blood. I touched my fingers gently to my forehead and probed the long gash running from my right temple to the left eyebrow.

The big man stated flatly, with no emotion, "That's a nasty knife cut chum. You'll need some stitches."

I blinked stupidly at him, but failed to tell him that it was not a knife cut. Broken glass had obviously been responsible for it.

Again he stated flatly, "You've been on some bender."

I sat there staring at him and said nothing. I was having difficulty orienting myself. It startled me to realize that I was not on my own boat. But after a moment I remembered falling to the deck of the fishing craft.

"Looks to me like you tried to take on a whole bar and got the living hell kicked out of you. Don't you guys ever learn?" He leaned over me, tilted my head back and examined the cut. "Tangle with a Mexican?"

"Well, I—"

"Looks like a Mexican job. Probably tried to slash across your eyes and got your forehead instead." He stepped back and asked, "You been fishing down in Mexican waters?"

Fishing? I looked down at my clothes and smiled weakly. I was dressed in blue canvas shoes, faded blue denim slacks and jacket, and a white and blue horizontally striped turtleneck sweater. Earlier I would have been recognized as a yachtsman, but I had lost my cap and the accident had changed my clothes to those of a shabby drunk who could have been in a barroom brawl and rolled in the gutter.

The mistake was amusing, in spite of the way I felt. I said, "Not exactly."

"But you're off some kind of boat."

I nodded, not knowing what to say and curious as to what was on his mind.

"Yeah." His interested expression changed to one of granite hardness. "Look, Mac, I didn't carry you down here because I like your looks. We need a cook. I noticed your soft hands, so it figured the only place you belonged on a boat was in the galley. How about it? Care to sign on?"

That was the oddest proposition I had ever had in my life. T. Howard Carleton, the third, asked to sign on a stinking fishing boat as ordinary cook to a bunch of morons. It was preposterously comical. It was even so good that I didn't care to spoil the moment, so I asked, "Where are you going?"

"Monterey. This is a shark boat. We've just been fishing off the Mexican coast, but Monterey is home port. We're on our way back." He crushed out his cigarette in a tin can nailed against the bulkhead, then said, "You think about it while I go for the first aid kit."

He turned away from me and scrambled up a steel ladder to the deck above. I propped my elbows on my knees and lowered my chin to my hands. I was feeling badly, with tom-toms in my brain, but I had evidently slept a few hours, since my clothes were dry and I was not as dazed as I had been. I tried to concentrate on the night's heavy drinking and certain incidents stood out. It had started earlier in the evening by running into Bunny's husband, Nicky, in a bar on the Sunset Strip. But Nicky had been a gentleman. No scenes for Nicky, even though he was facing the man who had been sleeping with his wife. Nicky was yellow.

Then there had been more bars and a private party somewhere and going to a strange woman's home for a nightcap. Of course, she had probably been primarily interested in the Carleton money, like everyone else, but I had a dim recollection that she had been exceedingly romp-worthy.

I pressed fingertips into my eyes and concentrated. Then I had the rest of it, scene by scene; Mimi snubbing me and learning that Bunny had been talking, thinking of Bunny and alcoholically getting angry about it and wondering what to do, and then the big, dramatic idea and borrowing the gun because firearms frightened her. The rest of it came back all too fast and all too ugly and Bunny was no longer the frightened one. Cold perspiration was heavy on my face and my spine was icy brittle with fear. I saw her again, the red life oozing out of her, and almost screamed. I bit my knuckles to stifle the scream and my mind spun crazily in nonsensical circles of blinding light. I had killed someone. An accident? Nevertheless, another human being was dead and I was the one who had pulled the trigger.

My mind could not accept the fact of that death and I twisted away to think again of the yacht and why I had been in such a hurry to get there. But the yacht was out as sanctuary. Even a moron could figure out where I had been heading when the wreck of the car was found. I thought that perhaps I had been lucky to land on the fishing boat.

I was thinking of it and wondering what the next step would have to be when the big fisherman returned with the first aid kit and a newspaper tucked under his arm. He seemed stupid to me; big, brawny, and powerful, but stupid. He tossed the paper on the bunk and examined my wounds for a moment. Then he swabbed the gash on my head with antiseptics, threaded a needle with surgical gut, and, before I realized what he had in mind or could protest, he pushed me back and began stitching the wound together. I almost fainted, but the pain itself acted as a sort of anesthetic. He gave me a drink of whisky out of a tin cup and that cleared my eyes, then held me steady while the bandage and adhesive tape were placed over the wound.

He stepped back and nodded approval of his own handiwork. "Not bad. That will keep. What's your name, Mac?"

Although I had been called Howard all my life, my first name was actually Thomas, after my father and grandfather. But I had never used Thomas. It would have been an impertinence. The first Thomas had been a man, all man. The old boy had arrived in California without a dime and, starting from scratch, had amassed a fortune in real estate and oil. And the second Thomas had not done badly. He had taken the original fortune and trebled it through sheer force of personality, brains, brawn, and skill. I, the last Thomas, did nothing. I spent the fortune.

But Tom seemed appropriate to a fishing boat and something was warning me not to give my right name. So I said, "Tom. And yours?"

"Matt Radovich. "

"Odd combination."

"I had a Slav father and an Irish mother. What's

your last name?"

I was about to reply when my eyes caught an item on the first page of the morning paper lying on the bunk. The paper was an extra with the headline: PROMINENT SOCIALITE MURDERED. Below that was the brief item, made even more horrible by its brevity:

LOVE-NEST MURDER

Mrs. Nicholas A. Holt, known to intimate friends and readers of the society columns as Bunny, was found dead at dawn this morning in her swank Beverly Hills apartment, allegedly a victim of foul play. The janitor of the building, noticing the door of the apartment open, investigated and found Mrs. Holt lying before her fireplace with a bullet through her heart. The murder weapon, a .45 Colt automatic pistol, was on the floor twenty feet away from the body, ruling out any possibility of suicide, according to the police. There was also considerable evidence that Mrs. Holt had been entertaining a visitor some time during the night.

Mrs. Holt leaves a husband, Nicholas A. Holt, who had recently started a divorce action against her, naming the fabulous sportsman and millionaire playboy T. Howard Carleton III, as correspondent. Mr. Holt was at his home, where he was stunned by the tragic news, but Mr. Carleton had not been located as this edition goes to press.

Further details will be forthcoming within the next few hours.

I swam up out of the black void in which I was drowning and stared at Matt Radovich. He seemed not to notice anything unusual in my expression. "Are you going to sit there reading the paper, or do you answer my question?"

I rubbed the dry tip of my tongue over sandpaper lips and asked hoarsely, "What question?"

"I asked you what's your last name?"

Fortunately all my senses had not come to a dead halt. I thought of a pet name I had been called as a child and said, "Howie. Tom Howie."

"Okay. Now look, I been fussing with you long enough. You booze hounds get in my hair, anyway. How about it? You signing on as a cook, or do I toss you ashore?"

I glanced down at the paper and my brain reeled with the effort of accepting the black words. But certain inescapable facts stood out with terrible clarity. Not only would the police find my fingerprints on the gun—probably had already—but it was a licensed gun, and Sammy Rubin would be questioned. Murder was not a thing to lie about. He would tell the truth, that I had been drinking and that I was obviously in an angry frame of mind. Another fact easily determined was that I had taken Bunny away from her husband but had tired of her. A third was a fact that a number of our friends knew that Bunny had tried to avenge herself. The reasoning, then, was simple—in the heat of my anger I had borrowed the gun with the deliberate intent of committing murder. There was only the one answer, cold-blooded and premeditated murder. Nothing I could say or plead would alter those bare facts. The highest priced staff of attorneys in the world could not change them. All of my millions were dead and lost to me.

I got up from the bunk and staggered into the head. When I returned to the forecastle the big fisherman was frowning at me and apparently about to change his mind. I was not exactly a choice item to have aboard.

I tried to compose my features and mumbled, "Sure, I can cook."

CHAPTER TWO

Matt wasted no more time, but beckoned me with a jerk of his head and started out of the forecastle. I followed him to the deck above, not knowing what to expect and caring less. I was as stupefied as an animal caught in the beam of a flashlight.

The superstructure on the main deck of the boat was a simple cabin containing the galley aft, a passage leading forward to the skipper's tiny combination stateroom and radio room on the port side and, forward of that, the cramped quarters of the wheelhouse. Above the wheelhouse was a small cabin with two surplus bunks and an open bridge for working the boat in harbor or while the nets were out. The galley, which was to be my headquarters, had a sink on the port side, a stove with burners and oven against the forward bulkhead and, in the aft starboard corner, L-shaped benches arranged around a small, rectangular table. Other than lockers and storage space under the benches, there was little else in the room. The rancid stench in the air was nauseating. The galley looked and smelled as if it had not been cleaned in years.

I washed my face and hands at the sink and ran a pocket comb through coal black hair before a small, chipped mirror nailed on the wall. I appraised the deep circles under my eyes and the bandage on my forehead, but was relieved that the night and the accident had left no greater damage. The Carleton features common to the family—a thin sensitive nose, faintly olive complexion, sensuous mouth, rounded chin, and high cheekbones were all intact. My body, wiry and slim, a fraction over six feet tall, had taken worse damage before and would soon forget the aches and bruises. In a week or so, I thought, I would look back on the present situation as something rare and unique, and worth recounting to my friends—with the proper embellishments, of course. Then I wondered, what friends? As if I ever had any.

Matt started showing me about the galley, pointing out where everything was located, when my attention was caught by the sound of someone pacing back and forth on the open bridge deck above. It sounded like a woman's high heels clicking on the deck.

Matt listened for a moment, too, then explained, "We have a passenger."

"You have a woman aboard this garbage scow?"

"Yeah. Ginny Norton. She's from Monterey, too. We're taking her home."

"What are you running here, a steamship line?"

"Geez, you'd think so. But Ginny's okay. Just had a

tough run of luck, is all. Like most well-stacked babes she thought she'd have a chance in Hollywood."

"Oh."

"Yeah, that's about it. She didn't make the grade. I ran into her in town yesterday and found out she was broke, so I offered her a bunk up above."

"She must be damned desperate to get on this tub."

"Aren't we all?"

"You got something there."

He turned the galley over to me and went forward to get out the crew. I knew how to operate the standard Shipmate stove and anticipated no trouble cooking simple meals. I had cooked on my own boat often enough when the crew had been sent ashore so I could be alone with special guests. I got the stove going, peeled and sliced potatoes, placed them in a shallow pan in the oven, and got out a huge slab of bacon to slice.

The crew came aft to the galley one by one while I was at work. The men were sour and bleary-eyed with hangovers. Tony was a dark, almost black Italian with a sullen mouth and suspicious, dangerous eyes. We disliked each other on sight. Pete was like a St. Bernard, shaggy, all hands and feet, and rather good-natured, even with a hangover. Johnson was a big, quiet Swede, a question mark. Nothing whatever could be read in his complete lack of expression. He gave me no more than a glance, accepting me as he would a piece of furniture. The attitude of the others was pretty much the same. They were simply not interested in me and cared only that someone was doing the cooking.

Oka Halversen, the blond Scandinavian skipper, came out of his cabin practically blind drunk. He was a surprise to me, as I had assumed that Matt was captain. The skipper could not have been older than forty, but deep marks of dissipation in his face added twenty years to his appearance. He staggered to the galley table, threw himself onto a bench, complained loudly of a bad hip, a bad night, and the bad crew, then grinned vacuously at me. "Pretty boy," he mumbled. "I tink ye got good cook." He gulped down a steaming cup of coffee, part of it slopping over his chin and running down his chest.

The girl came down from above and into the galley through the door leading to the aft deck, where all the nets and fishing gear were stacked. She paused in the doorway, frowning at me, the stranger, the breeze whipping her skirts about long, curved thighs. I turned around from the stove to appraise her and thought that Hollywood must be slipping. She was no great beauty, but every cell of her body radiated magnetism. Her hair was as black as mine and worn in the long page-boy style, tumbling loosely and thickly about her shoulders. Her eyes, too, were dark, almost pure black, but her skin was as white and smooth as cream. Her mouth, though bitter and sullen at the moment, was large and made for laughter and love. Her body was round and full, high-breasted, with a narrow waist and ample hips and altogether more womanly than a woman had a right to be. The outstanding characteristic, however, was the aura of sex that emanated from her.

It made itself felt in the room at once. The men

straightened their backs, stared at her, then looked uneasily at each other from the corners of their eyes. Only Tony glowered at her and looked away. Apparently, I thought, she had already given him the old brush-off.

She turned away from her curious study of me, shrugged a shoulder as if neither I nor anyone else was of interest to her, and made her way to the table with all the feline grace of a jungle cat. The men relaxed the moment she sat down and started talking with her about mutual friends in Monterey. It was obvious that all of them had known each other for many years. I soon gathered the information that the fishing industry had also played a large part in her background, as incongruous as it seemed.

I heard the diesel start up in the hold below, then Matt came into the galley. He smiled sketchily at the girl, but gave the skipper and crew a look of disgust on his way out to the aft deck. There was the slap of lines being taken from the wharf pilings and dropped on deck, then Matt returned to the galley, drank a quick cup of coffee, and went forward to the wheelhouse. While he had been present the whole crew had watched him, but no one had said a word. The engine throbbed into action, the screw thrashed white water, and the boat pulled away from the wharf and into the stream. We swung away from the docks and headed for the opening in the breakwater.

For a brief moment I toyed with the idea of leaving that boat in a hurry and running for my attorneys. They would know how to protect me. They had managed it more than once before. But could they protect me from a murder charge? That was doubtful. I had to think it out carefully before throwing myself on anyone's mercy, including my own attorneys. The fishing boat was the perfect sanctuary. I would have a few days, perhaps even a week, to regain perspective and do some intelligent planning in an atmosphere completely foreign to what I was used to. I decided to stay where I was.

Then Tony's voice rasped in my ears, "Well, we gonna sit here all morning, sweetheart?"

I turned my attention back to the cooking, dished out bacon and eggs and potatoes onto heavy crockery plates, placed them on the table, and refilled the coffee cups. I fixed a plate for myself, to help soothe my ragged nerves, and sat beside Johnson, diagonally across from Ginny Norton. She regarded me curiously for a moment but became more interested in the food. To my astonishment, I ate hungrily, even greedily.

Oka looked up from his plate and beamed happily about the table. "Good," he said. "Not grease all over like before. I tink you're all right, sveetheart."

"Why this sweetheart business?"

He chuckled. "Ve alvays call the cookie sveetheart."

He finished his plate, had two more eggs, then went forward to relieve Matt in the wheelhouse. Matt came back and took the skipper's place. He ate silently, his eyes fixed vacantly on space.

I watched the men and thought, Stupid, unthinking animals. Something was wrong with the boat and crew. No morale. No feeling of cohesion, of a group that has labored hard together and profited by their labors. No sharing of a common purpose. A drunken skipper and Matt, who seemed to dominate the whole outfit, with nothing but contempt in his eyes. It was a weird setup.

I looked over at Matt and asked, "Have you been having a bad season?"

Matt shrugged without looking at me, his mind on something else. But Tony put down his fork and snarled, "What's it to you?"

A cold shock ran up my spine. It was happening already. I turned toward the end of the table to look into Tony's hot eyes. "What a charming little animal. Were you simply whelped, or was your mother plowing at the time?"

Tony's face darkened another degree and his teeth gleamed yellow under a drawn lip. "I don't get that."

"Maybe we could do better in Esperanto."

"I don't know no foreign languages."

I choked over the coffee and laughed. Tony placed his hands flat on the table and leaned forward, ready to jump to his feet. The men were watching Tony, but Ginny Norton was looking at me, an interested light in her eyes. I appraised the danger in Tony's expression and cautioned myself to either keep quiet or change the subject and knew that I could do neither. I was suddenly tired and strangely exhilarated at the same time. It was the old story all over again. Always it was the same. That prodding into danger, asking for it, welcoming it, treading the same thin line and staring through the barrier of death.

"Esperanto," I explained, "is an artificial language devised so that simple-minded people like yourself may be able to converse with other ignorant and equally simple-minded people. Or do you fail to understand that, too?"

Tony said softly, "I don't like your looks, sweetheart. I think maybe I'll change 'em."

Matt said, "Leave him alone. He's in no condition to take you on."

I said, "On the contrary," and hooked my thumb in the heavy cup and flipped the hot coffee into Tony's face. He came up from the table roaring and screaming for blood. I had anticipated him and was already on my feet. I punched him on the side of the face with a quick left to knock him off balance back against the wall, then slugged him with a looping right. He went to one knee, with blood on his face, but bounced up as if he were made of rubber.

But after that it was no contest. Tony came at me and I was whipped before we had fairly started. He knew all the dirty tricks in the book and I was simply too weak and tired to counter them. He was rough and fast and rugged, but he was not really a good fighter and under normal circumstances I could have beaten him easily. But the night had taken too much out of me. Tony slugged with everything he had and in no time at all I was flat on my back. Tony then raised a foot to boot me in the face, but Matt grabbed him and tossed him to the far side of the galley.

"That's enough. Leave him alone."

Tony cried, "I'll kill the son of a bitch!"

Matt growled, "You make another move in his direction and I'll throw you overboard."

Tony glared at him, but knew it was hopeless to face down the bigger man. He stamped out of the cabin, muttering under his breath.

Matt helped me to my feet and tipped my head over the sink. Ginny joined us and bathed my nose with cold water until the bleeding stopped. Matt examined the bridge of my nose and grunted, "Broken." He went forward for a moment and returned with the first aid kit. He squeezed the bridge of my nose into place and plastered adhesive tape over the break. The ringing in my head stopped. I drank some cold water and felt better.

For the first time Matt smiled at me, a warm smile. He took my arm and walked me aft to the stern of the boat. We looked at San Pedro receding in the distance and down at the bubbling wake.

Matt leaned against the railing, lit a cigarette, then squinted at me. "You're a funny character, Tom. What made you tangle with Tony? You didn't have to bring that to a head."

I shrugged. "I don't like his type."

"Yeah. And he doesn't like yours. Better stay away from him. Tony can get damned dirty in the clinches." He blew out a cloud of smoke and shrewdly looked me up and down. "Another thing, you've never been with an outfit like this before. You know your way around a galley, but you're more careful and cleaner than a sea-going cook. And those clothes—I just noticed that's pretty expensive tailoring under that mud and oil. Just who are you and where the hell are you from?"

That was a question that could not be answered. I needed time to think of a background. I thought of the ignorant animals in the galley and glanced at the powerful giant at my side. He was curious about me, but, on the other hand, I felt that he was also willing to accept me without question.

That was proven correct when, after I failed to answer, he said, "Okay. It's none of my business. Anyway, I'm glad you're aboard. I guess you already noticed this is a pretty fouled-up boat. We're coming apart at the seams. But you—I got a hunch about you. I think you're the boy to bring things to a head."

That was an odd statement for him to make and I asked curiously, "Why?"

"I can't say, exactly. Sure, I know there's no sense to it, but I feel it." He was silent for a moment, then he chuckled and said, "Maybe it's because there's a little of the cornered rat in you."

"I beg your pardon."

"Yeah," he said, "I think that's it. You're the kind of character who'd spit in the warden's eye just to find out what solitary confinement was like. Yeah." He clapped me on the back with a heavy hand and burst into laughter. "You're just what this boat needs."

CHAPTER THREE

By the time we arrived in Monterey, a few days later, I was as filthy as the rest of the crew. In addition to the road oil on my clothes I had also acquired grease spots from the stove and smelled as rancid as the galley. Then there was the bandage on my forehead and the adhesive tape across the bridge of my nose. I looked as if I had been born and raised on that boat.

There was no further trouble with Tony during the journey and I learned what was wrong with the crew. Most of it centered around the skipper. Oka Halversen was one of the most skilled men in the shark business, but alcohol had got a grip on him during the past year. He was drunk most of the time. He had a wife living in San Diego, but he was also keeping a mistress in Monterey. I learned that Mrs. Halversen was not only unaware of the mistress but even thought her husband a teetotaler. It was a big joke with the crew. Where it interfered with their activities, however, was that the skipper preferred being ashore with his girlfriend and went fishing only when he ran out of money. The men worked on smaller shares than Oka so they were constantly broke.

Aside from Matt, though, the men seemed no better than the skipper. All of them had come from Monterey's big purse seine sardine fleet, but sardines had been running badly the past few years. Desperation had driven them from the purse seiners to Oka, and poverty kept them there. They were discouraged, irritable, hot-tempered, and, where spirit was concerned, beaten men.

Big Matt was different. He was something of an ichthyologist, had commanded a destroyer during the war and had been skipper and owner of his own seiner. The boat, however, had been lost to the bankers during the past bad season, so Matt had gone with Oka. He was there to learn the shark business and to mark time until he could go on his own again. He was a man of fast-changing and contradictory moods, but he was far from being beaten. In his light blue eyes was always the light of a bright future.

We acquired a rather odd liking, or perhaps tolerance, for each other. He knew I considered him mostly brawn and little brain, and I was well aware of the fact that he placed me somewhere between a spineless jellyfish and a rapacious barracuda that would eat its own young. My fight with Tony had not fooled Matt at all. He knew that courage had nothing to do with it. For which, I suppose, I should have credited him with better intelligence. But his size was against it.

Except for one occasion, I saw Ginny Norton only during mealtimes. She spent all her time in the tiny stateroom above, listening to platter programs on a portable radio. I could hear the music down in the galley at all hours of the day and most of the night. She had a rather indifferent friendliness toward Matt, but the rest of the gang she was obviously avoiding.

I stood my turn at wheel watch with the others, but the evening before we were due in Monterey I took the wheel on the open bridge deck above, rather than the one below. It was a cloudless night, made almost bright by a low moon and millions of stars, the sea was smooth and the bow was cutting away the watery miles. Off to my right was the shoreline, darker than the night. We were in close and I fancied that I could see the thin, white line of breakers against the shore.

The boat was steady on its course as I stood there at the wheel trying to resolve the turmoil in my mind. Contrary to what I had expected, I had been unable to work out any sensible course of action. Sooner or later, of course, I would have to call my attorneys and learn what they could do to protect me, if protection was possible. But I could not rely too heavily on them. They would need a plan to work on, a logical alibi of some kind. I had nothing to present to them other than the bare facts, and they were all weighted heavily against me. Yet, even without a plan, I would have to get in touch with them soon after reaching shore. I had no doubt that the police were combing the state for me. I could not afford to be picked up as a common criminal. It was also pretty obvious that I would not be able to hide out for long once I reached shore. The whole crew would know my identity within a day or two.

But the lack of a plan was not the only thing bothering me. I was also deeply immersed in self-disgust, as well as self-pity. I could find no particle of good in myself or anything that hinted toward a better and brighter future, even if I should get out of the mess I was in, which was highly improbable. I had to face, too, the fact that what had happened could easily happen again. The death wish that was driving me was as dangerous to others as it was to myself. Only a complete change in my habits of living could exculpate that danger, and that change I was not equipped to make.

I was turning it over in my mind when I felt someone approaching and turned about. Ginny had come out of her cabin and left the door open, so that the blaring music from the radio floated out into the night. She crossed behind me and leaned back against the railing on the seaward side of the bridge. She was wearing a pair of men's white nylon pajamas, furry slippers, and a robe thrown loosely over her shoulders. When she raised her hands to smooth back her hair her full breasts were sharply outlined in the moonlight.

"Cigarette?" she asked.

I handed her a package and some matches. She lit two cigarettes and handed one to me, casually putting the almost filled package in the pocket of her robe. I wanted to be alone and was annoyed with her presence but I had to smile. She had apparently run out of cigarettes, but would not ask anyone for a package, so had filched mine as if absent-mindedly putting her own away.

We stood there silently and I thought she would leave after a moment, now that she had what she wanted, but she showed no inclination to go. She looked beyond me toward the shore and, after a long while, sighed and said, "It's peaceful out here. Too bad we can't just drift this way forever, in the night, with the stars...." She shook her head and her eyes turned to me. "Isn't your name Tom?"

"That's right. No formal introductions on this tub."

"Oh, no one ever introduces anyone on a fishing boat. But all fishermen are that way. I know men who have fished together for years and all they know are each other's first names." She paused, then said bitterly, "My father was a fisherman. The business killed him finally. Killed my mother, too, trying to keep a home going and working in the canneries when the old man's pocket was empty, which was most of the time."

"You aren't exactly enthused about the business."

She said vehemently, "I hate it. Every part of it and

every man in it. I'd sink every boat in the fleet if I could." She blew a puff of smoke toward me, then said, "But you aren't part of it. I've been watching you down below."

"That so?"

"And listening to you. You don't talk like the others, except maybe Matt, a little. You've been educated somewhere."

I thought of the dozens of tutors and private schools and universities I had attended and said, "Here and there. But are all fishermen supposed to be uneducated?"

"Most of them. There's more than that, though. You're not a fishing cook. You're not sloppy enough; you keep things clean and you try to make the food appetizing."

"After all," I laughed, "I have to eat it, too."

"So do the others, but they don't care. You do. That's the difference. And you're polite—even to me."

"Shouldn't I be?"

She shrugged. "Oh, I don't know. Maybe. Maybe not." She let the thought hang in the air for a moment, then said, "Anyway, you're no fisherman. I've been around too many of them all my life not to know. I got a hunch you came out of a good background."

"Don't let it throw you. In many ways, my special background was as vicious as yours." I wanted to change the subject so I said, "Matt was telling me that you've been down south having a shot at the movies."

She flipped the cigarette stub overboard and watched it arc through the air down to the sea. After a long pause she looked back at me and nodded. Her voice was again bitter as she replied, "What a joke that was. You know something, Tom? Ever since I was sixteen people've been telling me I should be in the movies. Not just a few people, but almost everyone."

"You certainly have the curves in the right places."

"I know. That's it. I've been about Miss Everything on the Monterey Peninsula. All I ever had to do was put on a tight bathing suit and walk across a stage and the judges gave me the gold cup every time."

"As I say—"

"I know. I know. Curves. And sex. Plenty of it, they tell me. So I got convinced, saved my money, bought some decent clothes, and took off for Hollywood."

I glanced down at the compass, swung the wheel a degree on course, and asked her, "Want me to fill in the rest of it? You ran into third-rate greasy agents and the well-worn casting couch. Isn't that about it?"

She leaned closer to look into my eyes. "You know all about it, don't you?"

"A little. Am I right?"

"God, yes. You're so right. Oh, those slimy punks. Those homely little toads. And their filthy hands always reaching and pawing and grabbing and patting. I never got beyond an agent's office at any time. I never did see the inside of a studio. Friends, yes. Always they were introducing me to friends who were supposed to be somebody and taking me to luncheons and smelly cocktail parties and telling me how important they were and all the time angling me toward the most convenient bed."

"There are beds and there are beds."

She snapped, "What do you mean by that?"

"You could have worked your way up to the better beds."

"Why, you—"

"Most of them just wind up in bed, period, but some make the grade."

She sagged back against the railing and said, "I guess you're right. But I think I'd rather be a tramp. It's more honest."

I looked at her then, really looked at her, for the first time. She was bitter and seemed to be as beaten as the fishing crew, but that was an illusion. There was still spirit in her, a spark of something shining and better. She was no fool, and there was no doubt that she must have learned the various directions to take to find herself on the inside of a studio. She had, after all, but one commodity to sell and with a lush figure such as hers would not have had too much difficulty getting the right price for it. She would have had to work up through the toads and to the smoother operators, but, in the end, she probably could have made the grade. That she had refused to do so—she would not have been broke otherwise—made me regard her as a human being with some depth, rather than just a provocative body.

"Now," she said, "I'm really in for it. Gal goes away to make good, you know? And drags herself home like an alley cat. 'T'ain't funny."

"Why do you make yourself face it?"

She smoothed down the pajama jacket and pulled the robe tighter about her shoulders. "I was born and raised in Monterey. I'm known. I can get an honest job there without a bed being part of the pay. That's for me. I'll put up with the rest of it."

"And some day you'll marry a handsome, young fisherman and work in the canneries."

Her shoulders twitched and she shuddered as she turned and walked away from me. She paused a moment to look back at me and said, "Never. Believe me, that is something that will never happen. I'd die first."

I heard the cabin door slam behind me and looked out over the dark sea cut by the silver path of the moon. I shrugged, too, and thought, To hell with it. She means nothing to me.

We docked in the morning at Monterey's fishermen's wharf. As soon as the boat was made secure I went ashore with Matt. On the two sides of the old wooden wharf, and running its entire length, were stalls for selling fish, wholesale sheds for buying, a couple of curio shops, boat equipment shops, beer and soft drink counters, and a large number of seafood restaurants. The place bustled with activity and the excited jabber of Portuguese and Italian.

Apparently everyone knew Matt. Wherever we went he was greeted with a wave and broad smiles and friendly, vigorous handshakes. He was not only well known, but, more important, was well liked. It was an unusual experience for me to be with a person who was liked so openly and so heartily. And because I was with him I was included in the atmosphere of general good feeling. That was an even odder experience.

We went to Angelo's, a garishly painted restaurant on the wharf, and sat on padded barrels before the beer and wine counter. The bartender warmly shook hands with Matt, then shoved some cold beer toward us. He grinned and said, "On the house." Matt drank his beer out of the bottle, so I emulated his example.

Ginny came in with two heavy suitcases and an overnight make-up kit. She asked the bartender if it would be all right to leave them with him for a while, so he put them in a corner behind the bar. She sat down between Matt and me and accepted a beer from the bartender. She then leaned toward Matt to whisper in his ear, but I overheard her.

"I hate to ask," she told him, "but I don't have a cent. Would you lend me twenty dollars, Matt? I'll pick up a job today or tomorrow, get an advance, and pay you back right away."

Matt's face turned red. "Geez, I'm damned sorry, Ginny, but I only have a few bucks in my pocket. I won't have any more till we get the shark livers shipped off. If that will do you any good, later this afternoon—"

I took a twenty-dollar bill from my wallet and placed it on the bar before Ginny. She looked down at it and bit her lip, her own skin changing color slightly. It was obvious that she wanted to refuse, but after a moment she picked up the bill, folded it neatly, and placed it in her purse.

She mumbled, "Thanks," so softly that I could barely hear her. "I—I'll pay you back tomorrow or the next day."

"Forget it. There's no hurry."

"Just a regular little old millionaire, aren't you?"

Matt chuckled and said, "Certainly Tom's a

millionaire. Didn't you know? He just cooks on stinking fishing boats because he loves the work."

I looked around at him, but he was smiling at Ginny and I could not read his expression. She thanked me again, touched Matt's arm with her fingertips, and left the room with a provocative sway of hips that could have meant a fortune in any box office. Matt took a swallow of her untouched beer and passed the bottle to me. Letting good beer go flat was evidently not the thing to do.

"She's okay," he said, as if I had asked.

"Can she get a job as easily as she thinks?"

"Hell, yes. She's a cocktail waitress. Any bar owner in town would give his right arm to have her in his place. Figure it out yourself. Wherever she works, that's where every young buck in town will hang out, and the older bucks, too. She'll pick her spot and have a job in less than an hour."

"Quite a body."

"That's no lie." He wiped his mouth with the back of his hand and grinned broadly at me. "Like everybody else, I made a play for her a few years ago. Looked okay, at first, I guess she kind of liked me, but I didn't get to first base. The minute I made a pass that ended it. Geez, can you imagine what it would be like to hit the sack with a gal like that?"

"Very easily. But someone must have made the grade."

"By God, I don't know! I've been watching her ever since she was worth watching and I still don't know. Of course, I've heard characters brag about it, but you know what liars most of them are. And right now they aren't so apt to shoot off their mouths. You see, she almost killed a guy last year."

"Really?"

"Sure. The way it happened, I guess she likes swimming in the nude. There's a secluded cove down below the Highlands where she used to go. She thought it was a safe spot, but this obnoxious character accidentally discovered it. So one day he hides down there in the rocks with a telescopic lens on a good camera and snaps a dozen pictures of her. Then he blew them up, printed them, and sold them for ten bucks a set."

I had to laugh and said, "I'll bet he did a landslide business."

"He sure did! You can imagine, with a figure like hers. But a friend of hers got hold of one of the sets and gave them to Ginny, with the guy's name and address. She got a pistol somewhere and went over there and started squeezing off bullets. Fortunately, she didn't hit him and the guy managed to dive through a window. She found the negatives and destroyed them and proceeded to tear his apartment to pieces. If the police hadn't arrived I think she would have burned the place down. Some temper when she gets going. Irish father and an Italian mother."

"Nothing happened to her?"

"Oh, no. The cops killed the whole thing themselves, as long as she promised not to take another shot at the guy. Naturally, though, a lot of people think she really posed for those pictures, so she isn't exactly welcomed in the better social circles around here. In fact, she doesn't do too well in any circle. Other women either hate her, or, if they have a husband hanging around, they're afraid of her. It's that come-on look that does it. That's probably the big reason why she wanted to get away and went down south."

"But, then, the fact that she has come back doesn't make much sense. She could probably have got a job as a waitress there."

"Yeah, I know. She told me about it. But in the line she's in, she can make better money here. I suppose there are other reasons, too." He paused a moment, then squinted at me and asked, "What's the answer, Tom?"

"Ginny? Why, I hardly know her—"

"No, no. Not her. I mean us."

"But what's the answer to what? Maybe I had better hear the question first."

"Okay. Are you staying with us, or not? You're no Antoine, but at least your cooking isn't greasy, and that's saying a lot on a fishing boat."

I was inclined to laugh in his face but said, "I'm not really a cook."

"You're telling me? But we don't use a full-time cook, anyway. On a fishing boat a man is a fisherman first and a cook incidentally. You do better than most of them, and I've noticed you know boats. I can teach you how to handle the nets."

I was still feeling confused and didn't care to break from him right at that moment, so I asked, "What is there in this shark business?"

"Plenty, if you hit it right. We catch soup-fin sharks in gill nets, for their livers. Most of your vitamin A comes from shark liver, you know. The male liver runs around ten dollars a pound. Shark liver is about one-tenth of the weight of the fish, so with a sixty-pound soup-fin shark that means sixty bucks per fish. The female livers are low in vitamin A and bring in about a buck a pound. But when they have pups the content runs higher than a male's, up to about fourteen bucks a pound."

"What do you do with it?"

"Well, we put the livers in five-gallon cans, forty pounds to the can. Then we ship it up to a laboratory in San Francisco for vitamin appraisal and, after that, sell it at auction to the pharmaceutical houses. We also sell the carcasses to wholesalers and, of course, the ventral fins sell to the Chinese for soup. It's good soup, by the way."

"Want me to cook some for you?"

He laughed and said, "Seriously, Tom, I'd like you to stay aboard. We're going to set our nets off Point Sur in a few days. I guarantee you'll get sharks down there. If we do you'll have a nice stake for yourself."

I thought of the money in my wallet, at least twenty hundred-dollar bills and some smaller currency, and of the Carleton controlled banks and oil fields. I managed to keep from laughing and said, "It's tempting."

Matt lifted his bottle and drained the balance of the beer down his throat. He called for more beer and turned back to me. Amused lines tugged at the corners of his mouth, but his blue eyes were shrewd and knowing. "No," he said, "it isn't tempting. Not the money. I got a hunch you're a little careless about money. You didn't think to ask what you were getting paid on the boat."

"Then why—"

"I think something else might tempt you. Yourself."

I finished my beer and lifted the second bottle. "How do you mean that?"

He shrugged. "It's hard to say. I can't put my finger on it. But I don't think you know who you are." I started to say something, but he frowned at me and said, "I mean it. You're a fouled-up character if I've ever seen one. Maybe this is your chance to learn something about yourself. Anyway, it's worth thinking about."

I looked into his eyes and nodded. "Maybe."

He sniffed at a sudden scent of perfume in the air and turned to look over his shoulder. The hard lines at the corners of his eyes faded, the thin line of his mouth dissolved into an awkward grin, and there was color flooding into his cheeks. It looked suspiciously like a blush, though that was hard to believe.

The girl was standing directly behind us, smiling warmly at Matt. She put out her hand as he got clumsily to his feet and her smile became something really beautiful. Whatever else she may have been to Matt, she was certainly a friend. But that was no surprise; he seemed to be everyone's friend. What did amaze me was that he should even know someone like her.

She was rather tall, somewhat over medium height, but seemed even taller by virtue of her long, slim legs and a slender, though well-rounded, body. Her dark brown hair, reflecting occasional auburn tints from the light, hung just to her shoulders and turned under in a short page boy. It had a center part and curled back over her round temples in two long waves. It was obviously an expensive coiffure and one requiring constant attention. It was so well done and so meticulously precise that I had an almost uncontrollable urge to reach out and disarrange it. I managed to stifle that.

Her eyes were large, widely spaced, and dark brown, flecked with amber lights. Even as she smiled she was careful not to squint too much. The balance of her features made excellent composition; rather wide cheekbones, a full mouth, a thin nose that made her profile seem like an etching, a faultlessly smooth and well-tanned complexion, and a rounded chin that just slightly suggested ample will power. She was wearing an expensive Adrian suit of some checked material, with matching shoes, evidently Delman's, and was carrying a matching bag. The ensemble was as precisely correct as her coiffure.

I don't like instant appraisals of people, but my reaction to her was that she was a person of many contradictions. She was apparently vain, yet her smile denoted a fund of unusual warmth. She was beautiful and obviously knew it, yet that beauty lacked assurance. She searched for approval in the mirrors of other people's eyes. Then, too, there was something frantic about the very correctness of her hair and dress and make-up. Either something was lacking, or, what I later learned to be correct, she suffered from the constant fear of the possibility of "overdoing," as she expressed it. Even so, under the bright *Vogue* and *Harper's* surface, I could sense a real person. In spite of my first snap judgment, I rather liked her.

She paid absolutely no attention to the fact that we were greasy, filthy, and smelled to high heaven of fish and a rancid galley. She ignored it. She put an arm around Matt and hugged him with no wrinkling of the nose or any expression of distaste, even though her thin nostrils must have been horrified.

"I ran into Ginny a minute ago and she told me where you were," she said to Matt. "It's good to see you back. You've been gone too long."

He smiled as broadly as a schoolboy and nodded. "Seven months."

"Any luck?"

"Oh, a little. We sent some cans up from Central America, but it wasn't so good off Mexico."

"But you've done better than the men here. You know, this place is going to collapse if the sardines don't come back. Can't you bring them back, Matt? You're big enough to wade out in the sea and drive them all to shore."

"Not that big," he chuckled.

I asked, "Is fishing so important here?"

"Without it," she said, "Monterey is a dead port. It's the only industry we have." Then she really noticed me for the first time. "Are you a stranger here?"

Matt looked embarrassed and hurried to introduce us.

Her name was Gail Norton, Ginny's cousin. Matt also passed the casual information that he and Gail had been practically raised together, though he was older.

"Howie," she said thoughtfully. "Tom Howie. There's

something familiar about your name. Oh, I know," she smiled. "You have the first two initials and almost the same names as T. Howard Carleton, the man all Los Angeles is looking for." She looked amused as she said, "I don't suppose you're related to him."

I dropped back to the barrel seat at the bar and had a sip of beer. When I was over the surprise of hearing my own name, I said, "Never heard of him."

"Oh, now, you must have. After all, that's one of the most powerful names in the West."

She started to turn back to Matt, but I asked, "Why is everyone looking for him?"

"They're really searching for his body. He ran off some highway down south and into the water. His car was found but not his body. They're dragging for it."

I shuddered as an icy chill ran up my spine. I had not thought of that possibility.

Gail sighed and told Matt, "Just my luck. Another eligible bachelor gone. Why couldn't I have met him? He can't use all that money anymore, and I could."

I stared at her. The statement had not been made lightly. There had been too much yearning and frustration in her voice. She meant it. I noticed the way Matt was regarding her, with a resigned expression, and picked up another clue to her character. "Another eligible bachelor gone," was the main key to her whole make-up.

I got up from the bar and told Matt, "See you later. I have something to do."

He grabbed my arm in a viselike grip. "Wait a minute. You're not running out on me, are you?"

"No. I'll be back."

"Here?"

"Well—"

"Look, I have some business to attend to, too. Suppose you meet me back here at five, this afternoon."

"That's all right."

"Good. See you then."

I asked him how to get into town, and he replied, "Just follow the wharf to the main street and that's it."

Gail offered to accompany me. I did not care for her company, but could hardly refuse the offer. We left Angelo's together and started down the wharf toward town. Gail chattered away about Monterey, but I was preoccupied and paid little attention. I did notice, however, that she seemed to know as many people as Matt. She smiled lightly and nodded at practically everyone we passed. The men, without exception, swiveled their necks to look after her and scowled at me, the stranger.

We left the wharf, crossed the railroad tracks, and went around the corner of the old customs building to Alvarado, the main street. Gail stayed with me until we were in the middle of town, a walk of but a few minutes. I spotted a small hotel near one of the theatres and decided to check in so I could use a telephone with some privacy.

I stopped in front of the hotel and told Gail, "I'll be leaving you here."

She was not at all pleased with my abrupt departure. "So soon? But I haven't learned anything about you. You've been so silent. And, after all, any friend of

Matt's—"

Even me, I thought, with a bandage on my forehead, adhesive tape across my nose, filthy clothes, and smelling of a fishing boat galley. It was a compulsion with her. Every man she met had to fall in love with her, or at least approve. What she thought of the man was nothing. What he thought of her was the most important thing in the world.

I thought, Holy God, and said, "I'm in a hurry, darling. I'll tell you how gorgeous you are some other time. I promise."

She stepped back and stared at me as if I had lost my senses, but she didn't argue. She twisted about, turned on her heel, and left me standing there. I watched her walk up the street and thoroughly approved. The only other person who could walk like that, with exactly that proper suggestive sway of the hips, was Ginny. I couldn't help but approve.

Next to the hotel entrance there was a newsstand that carried Los Angeles papers. I bought one, then went into the tiny lobby of the hotel. The place looked cheap and rundown, but at least it was clean. The elderly clerk sniffed and stared at me suspiciously over the rim of his glasses. I paid for the room in advance and mentioned that I was going to make a long-distance call. He made me leave a ten-dollar deposit to cover that.

I had no baggage to be carried, so I went up alone to the second floor and a small, neat room overlooking the street. I sat on the edge of the bed and opened the first page of the paper and found nothing. What I was seeking was on the second page:

BODY OF T. HOWARD CARLETON III
STILL NOT FOUND

The harbor police and Coast Guard are diligently dragging the waters of the San Pedro estuary for the body of the millionaire sportsman, T. Howard Carleton III; believed lost in a highway accident last Friday night or early Saturday morning. There has yet been no sight of the body either in the estuary or in the harbor, which is also being searched. According to the authorities, it is possible that the body may have been carried out to sea.

Mr. Carleton's British sports car, a convertible Jaguar, was found Saturday morning almost wholly beneath the waters of the estuary. Evidently he had been on his way to his yacht, the famous *Lucinda*, which is moored in the San Pedro harbor. According to the police reconstruction of the accident, Mr. Carleton must have been traveling at great speed, failed to make a turn, skidded, turned over three times, and crashed down the bank into the estuary. Blood was found on the road and the left doorframe.

That the accident was fatal is fairly certain as there were no footsteps leading to the road from the wreck of the car, or any other indication that Carleton may have crawled up the muddy bank. He is believed to have perished in the wreck and his body washed out to sea by the tides.

The well-known flyer, polo player, and yachtsman was the last male of a family that has made a great and lasting imprint on the State of California. In addition to Carleton controlled banks, land offices, and vast real-estate holdings, Mr. Carleton owned huge oil interests in California, Oklahoma, and Texas and, for years—

That was enough. I shoved the paper aside, reached for the telephone, and asked the downstairs clerk to get long distance. As soon as I had the operator I gave her the number of my attorneys' offices in Los Angeles, then sat back to wait.

But when the operator said pleasantly, "If you hang up, please, you will be called when the connection is made," I had a much better idea.

I said, "Cancel it."

"Sir?"

"Cancel the call. I don't want it."

"Very well."

I put the receiver on the hook and stared at the wall with a feeling of mounting excitement. For the moment, at least, Carleton was dead. He could stay that way for weeks, or perhaps months, or possibly forever, without danger. The body would not be found and the police blotter on the case would be closed. No one would be looking for me—alive.

But if I returned what could I expect? Certainly a trial. And a trial in which it would be ridiculous to expect any jury to believe my story that the shooting had been accidental. That I had inadvertently pulled the trigger while passing out was easy enough to understand, but it was too pat to be believed. No juryman would like to think of himself as being quite that naive. So only one of two results could come of such a trial, life imprisonment or the gas chamber.

Regardless of the fact that I felt morally responsible for Bunny's death, I could not face either result.

Tom Howie, though, newly created cook on a fishing boat, was very much alive. As Tom Howie, I had somewhat of a chance to live and to start all over again. No one would bother me, no one would cater to me, and no one would flatter me or lie to me because of my name. I would be one of the faceless millions and accepted as such. I might even learn to live with myself.

Tom Howie, I thought, fisherman. Not bad. It might work. And if it did not? I shuddered as an icy chill traveled up my spine.

CHAPTER FOUR

I had the clerk send up a bottle of bourbon and poured a straight shot in a water glass I found in the bathroom. I had another, then took the bottle and glass into the bedroom, and sat in a rocker by the window to look out over the town's main street. The air was so clear that I could see over the low buildings across the street and to the mountains beyond the Salinas Valley. The Carletons had once owned extensive holdings in the produce fields and loading sheds of Salinas, but I had sold them out some years before.

One of the biggest men in the produce game had borrowed heavily to buy me out. When it came time to sign the contracts I flew up to see him and remained as his house guest for a week. He was a powerful, rugged individualist with a much younger and fairly attractive wife. So I made an obvious and open play for the wife, wondering what he would do about it. He did nothing. There was too much at stake in the deal. I have never seen a man suffer as much misery as he, but he did nothing. The money involved in the deal had been more important than his wife or his pride.

I thought of how it had been, then thought of Bunny and Nicky. I had helped that affair along, too, wondering how it would turn out and what each of them would do about it. She had been after the Carleton fortune, had used every trick in the book, had burned her own bridges, and had even put herself in a position of public ridicule, without ever jockeying me into the desired position.

Now, I realized, I had paid too much attention to my own role and not enough to the dangerous one Bunny had been playing. She had gone beyond the point of no return and had left only the satisfaction of revenge. It was sickening to realize that I had pushed her to that point. Even more frightening, however, was the fact that my manner of living could cause it to happen again.

I worked on the bottle of bourbon in the small hotel room and tried to peel away the surface layers to discover just what kind of person I really was. What little I found was not pretty. I had never worked seriously at anything in my life, I had far too much time and money, too many people catered to me, and I was inclined to be patronizing and suspicious of everyone. That I had for a long time been subconsciously or even consciously disgusted with myself was as inescapable a reality as the death wish which had such a strong hold on me. But I could go no deeper. Self-flagellation was also not my nature.

The stinking clothes I was wearing finally turned my mind to other matters. I left the hotel to search for a men's shop and found a good one just up the street. I bought a complete change of clothes and found a gabardine suit that fitted me as if it had been tailored, which was surprising. It was the first suit I ever owned that hadn't been tailored. I paid for the purchases, tipped the clerk for a rush job, bought some necessities in a drugstore, and took a little walk around town. When the suit cuffs had been altered I picked it up and went back to the hotel, where I shaved and soaked in the tub, then dressed in clean clothes. I felt as if I had been reborn. Another heavy slug of bourbon and I was ready to go out.

I took a long walk around Monterey, the first capitol of California, and tried to interest myself in the squat adobe buildings of the early settlers. The town was an odd mixture of the neon-lighted and garish modern and the early graciousness of the *vaqueros*, but it had a certain charm that was appealing. Most of Alvarado Street, however, was strictly honky-tonk; shooting galleries, too many cheap bars, card rooms, cheap curio and servicemen's shops, and all kinds of clip joints catering to the soldiers of nearby Fort Ord and the men of the fishing fleet. But the ever-present blue waters of Monterey Bay and the clean sweep of the curving beach beyond alleviated the harshness and cheapness of that end of town.

My interest in the town was not that of a tourist. I

had been there before. I was simply killing time while arguing with myself over the decision I had made.

I walked down Alvarado and entered a bar not far from the wharf. Johnson and Pete, from the shark boat, were seated at the bar drinking beer. They turned to regard me with the blank, bovine curiosity of animals as I came in, then jerked their heads at me. My scrubbed appearance and the new clothes must have surprised them, but they made no comment. I dropped onto a stool next to Johnson and ordered a highball with bonded whisky.

Pete squinted at me and asked, "You got paid?"

I wondered why he asked, then realized that bonded whisky was beyond the reach of poverty-stricken fishermen. I said, "I had a little money." And lied, "Won it in a crap game in San Diego."

That satisfied them and also seemed to explain my new clothes. But when I offered to buy them a drink they shook their heads. Johnson said, "We can't buy back." There was something dignified about the way he said it, so I didn't press him. It was odd, though, that men in their condition could retain even the slightest shred of dignity, I thought.

In spite of my confused state of mind, I began to relax in their company. They wanted nothing and demanded nothing. They accepted me as a person, not as a symbol, and they talked freely before me. I learned that they were married men with large families living in Monterey and that they were reluctant to go home. They sipped slowly at their beer and in their eyes was the pain and hurt of how they were going to explain the all too few dollars they were bringing to their families. Rents were overdue, bills were piling up, credit had long since been gone, and they had their children to face, who simply needed ordinary clothes for school.

Pete grunted and said, "I don't know, Swede. It's got me."

Johnson snorted, "Yeah."

"The car's been gone a year, we lost the washing machine and the radio, I can't even pay school lunches for the kids and—and—I don't know." He shook his head as would a wounded animal at bay. "If only Oka would fish."

"Boozer."

"He knows how to get shark. We could make some dough."

"He could get 'em if he wanted."

"So could Matt. He's learned the business now. He's got the head on him and he wants to fish. Only it ain't his boat."

"It ain't Oka's neither. He charters it."

"I know. But he's got it. That's the thing. When you got it you're in, and Matt ain't got it. And they're Oka's nets."

"That's the main thing. You own all the boats in the world and they're no good without nets."

He clenched and unclenched his big fists on the bar. "Geez, if only Matt had the nets and the boat."

"We'd get shark then, for sure."

"My God, yes."

They lapsed into silence, staring moodily into space, burdened with problems that neither of them could solve. That they could undoubtedly make a better living elsewhere had probably never entered their minds. They were fishermen. Fish were out there in the ocean to be caught and they knew how to do the catching. That was all they did know. I felt embarrassed and turned my attention to the barroom.

It was a small room with booths against two walls, leather chairs and oak tables near the entrance, and a closed horseshoe-shaped bar against the back wall. There were perhaps twenty people in the room at the time. Most of them were silent, staring into their glasses as if they were crystal balls, the manner of bar customers the world over. They were at the lower end, yet on the same level with the rest of our saloon-civilization. Their attitude was really no different than the white-tie set in the elegant supper clubs.

While I was watching them their heads came up, their backs straightened, and false smiles appeared on most of the faces. I glanced toward the door and saw Gail Norton entering the room. But it was not Gail on whom they were turning their servile smiles. It was the man with her.

He was a ruddy-faced individual with small and shrewd, but laughing eyes, wirelike red hair, a barrel chest, and the sloping shoulders of a man who could have done well in the prize ring. He wore a king-size diamond ring on his left hand, his tie and shirt were obviously custom-made, and his double-breasted suit could have come only from the hands of an excellent tailor. He looked like a self-made man who had come up the hard way and was thoroughly enjoying his success. He also appeared to enjoy flaunting that success before others. His hearty manner was more than a little patronizing and annoying.

They walked to the curve of the bar just opposite us. Gail nodded at Pete and Johnson, and looked curiously at me for a moment before remembering. She gave me a cool nod and turned to smile at the man with her. I looked at the curve of her back, the well-rounded hips, the long, slender legs, and wondered what she was doing with the red-headed ape.

He slapped some bills down on the bar and called to the beaming bartender, "Okay, Joe, same as usual. Best Scotch in the house and keep your thumb out of the glass." He laughed as he watched the Scotch being poured, then glanced around at the rest of the customers, and boomed heartily, "You may as well set 'em up for all my friends. You know me." Then he saw me across the bar and mumbled, "All except that guy over there. I don't know him."

Johnson looked across at him and drawled, "Then we don't drink neither. He's with us."

The redhead frowned at us, but in a moment he was laughing again. "My mistake, Swede. I thought the guy was a stranger."

"He come with us on the shark boat."

The redhead cocked an eyebrow at me. "He sure don't look it."

Gail whispered, "Doesn't."

"Yeah. Doesn't. See what he'll have, Joe. Can't afford to make mistakes around here. These boys don't bring me fish, I go out of business. Ain't that the truth?"

Gail whispered, "Isn't."

"Yeah, honey. It's sure the truth. Well, boys, drink hearty. It's a short life and a merry one, I always say."

As soon as the bartender had mixed drinks for everyone the redhead lost interest in the customers. He turned away, his head close to Gail, for a mumbled conversation. He was evidently trying to sell her something, since she kept shaking her head, though the steady smile remained fixed.

I asked Johnson, "Who is he?"

Johnson whispered, "Steve Moore. He's one of the big guns on Cannery Row. Owns the Moore-Ellsberg Cannery."

I had a hunch and asked, "What happened to Ellsberg?"

Johnson's expression did not change, but twinkling lights appeared in his eyes. "You guessed it. Moore cut his throat last year and eased him out. Now he owns the works."

"Rugged character?"

"Yeah. He ain't no pantywaist."

Pete leaned over to whisper. "He's big cheese during sardine season. Dictates all the contract terms. The other canners go his way or else. We ever get another good sardine season, he'll be a millionaire." He paused in thought, then said, "I'd kinda hate to see it happen."

Johnson grunted, "Me, too."

"Where does Miss Norton fit in?"

"Can't you figure that one?" Then Pete gave me his good-natured grin. "I keep forgetting you're a stranger. Well, he's on the make, but she's out for a ring and a license and that sweet music. Moore ain't never been married and don't like the idea, but I bet she makes the grade."

I could not hide my astonishment. "But hell, man, I

should imagine a character like Moore would grab such a beautiful woman as Miss Norton."

Pete shook his head. "You don't know the score. There's two Miss Nortons in the picture."

"Her cousin Ginny?"

"Yeah. Moore's kinda nuts about her, too."

Johnson mumbled, "Who ain't?"

"But," I said, "this Gail Norton certainly must be far above Moore's social level. What is her interest in him?"

Pete scratched at his chin, then leaned closer to me to whisper, "It's kinda complicated. Gail's old man and old lady were killed in an automobile accident year before last. He owned the big Norton cannery, so Gail inherited it."

Johnson said, "She doesn't know how to operate it."

Pete nodded in agreement. "Yeah, that's part of it. She can't run the plant and the managers steal her blind, but we've had bad seasons, too, and she's lost plenty money. Matt says she's almost broke and maybe she'll lose the works. So she's making a play for Steve Moore."

"I'm beginning to see the light."

"Uh-huh. He's big stuff. Got a lot on the ball. Bulls his way through anything. So if he married her he'd have to pull her plant out of the red, too, and maybe combine it with his own. That way Gail'd be back on her feet again. You see?"

"Very clearly."

Johnson snorted, "I don't like her. Always putting on a phony front, getting her name in the papers, and running around with the big shots alla time."

Pete shrugged. "Well, maybe she's got the right idea. What the hell, Swede, who are we to say? Can you blame a good-looking babe for wanting to stay on top? I could just see myself hanging around with some stinking fisherman if I was a woman with a figger like hers. She ain't dumb."

"Huh!"

"Why is it," I asked, "that you accept a drink from Moore and wouldn't take one from me?"

Johnson growled, "Friends."

Pete said, "Moore likes to play big shot and, anyways, he can afford it. You're one of us. That's different."

I lifted the second highball and stared into the amber liquid, feeling strangely moved. Friends. One of us. For the first time in my life I was in a situation where nothing out of the ordinary was expected of me. No one was seeking my favor. No one intended patting me on the back. I was not expected to pick up nine checks out of ten and had been counseled, at least by inference, to keep my money in my pocket. I was considered no better and no worse than the men I was drinking with. However I was considered in their eyes depended solely on myself as an individual and not what I represented.

It was a unique experience, something that had never happened to me before. I was so intrigued by the idea that I did not notice Moore and Gail leaving until they were almost to the door. Then I turned about and called, "Just a minute, Mr. Moore."

He glanced irritably at me, one eyebrow raised in a question. "Something on your mind, chum?"

"Yes. You bought me a drink. I would like to return

the favor."

He was startled for a moment. Evidently he was not used to having the score of his largesse balanced by a fisherman. He squinted at me thoughtfully, appraised my clothes and the bandages on my face, and smiled thinly.

"Kind of stepping out of your class, ain't you?"

I had not been especially interested in him and had offered to buy the drink only out of normal courtesy, but his attitude aggravated me. I returned his smile. "We are all little children before Bacchus."

"I don't drink with no little children." He threw his head back and roared at his own joke, also winking at the other bar customers and slapping Gail on the back.

I said, "I insist."

His expression sobered instantly to a dark scowl. "Yeah? How come?"

Gail looked at me narrowly, but she was still smiling that fixed smile. "His mother probably told him never to accept gifts from strangers. But it's all right, Steve. I have a little time yet."

I called the bartender and ordered another round of drinks for the house. Gail and Moore stood at the bar by my side. She watched me from the corner of her eyes, slyly and curiously. Moore faced squarely toward me, scowling down at me. It pleased me, in a small way, to notice the bewilderment growing in his eyes. He could not catalogue and file me away neatly.

"New around here?" he asked.

"Yes."

"I'm Steve Moore, Moore-Ellsberg Cannery."

"So I've been told. I'm Tom Howie."

He nodded but did not offer to shake hands. He gulped down his drink and, though Gail's had hardly been touched, shoved her glass aside. He took her arm and rudely turned her away from the bar.

He dropped a patronizing hand on my shoulder and patted my back. "Stay with the sharks, chum. Stay with the sharks."

"Why?"

"Because," he said and grinned, "if you go with the sardine fleet you're getting in my territory and I got a hunch I wouldn't like that. Y' know? I wouldn't like it at all. Understand?"

I glanced at the other customers in the bar, all of them silent and frozen and watching me curiously. I turned back to Moore and said, "Perfectly."

He chuckled and waved at the others and escorted Gail to the door. There he paused and looked back at me with a broad smile that was nevertheless vicious. Why he had taken such an instant dislike to me I couldn't figure out, but I suppose I had violated his code. By repaying his favor in kind I had lowered him from the big shot level to just another customer buying a drink.

He chuckled and said, "Be seeing you."

I nodded and said pleasantly, "You certainly will, my friend—in the sardine fleet."

Blood rushed to his temples and for a moment I thought he was coming after me, but Gail had him by the arm and was whispering in his ear. Muscles twitched in his jaws and he stared at me as if he would like to tear me limb from limb. Gail's whispering, however, turned the tide. He glared at me a moment longer, then shrugged, attempted a forced laugh, and went out the door with Gail. Practically every man in the bar slowly let out his breath.

Johnson scowled at me and sniffed, "You ain't got much sense."

Pete leaned over the bar and laughed. When he looked at me there was respect in his eyes. "I wouldn't like to be in your shoes," he said, "but I'm glad you done it. Boy, he didn't like you nohow. Old big shot hisself gotta stand at the bar and take a drink from an ordinary fisherman. Oh, brother!" He went off into loud gales of laughter.

I glanced at my watch, finished the drink and got up from the stool. It was time to meet Matt. I slapped Johnson and Pete on the back and walked out of the saloon, conscious that everyone was watching me.

Matt was not at Angelo's. As I walked up to the bar the bartender asked, "You the guy was with Matt Radovich this morning?" When I nodded, he said, "Tom Howie, huh? Well, Matt called a minute ago and said you was to meet him on the boat."

I walked clown the wharf to the shark boat warped in against the pilings and for the first time noticed its name, the *Rosita*. I went down a steel ladder, dropped to the deck, and walked into the cabin. Matt was seated on a bench before a pile of papers scattered over the galley table. He had shaved and taken a bath and changed to slacks, a flannel shirt, and a short suede jacket, the kind affected by motorcycle fanatics. He looked bigger than ever and even sitting down seemed to fill the room.

He glanced at me with an angry expression loaded

with frustration. "What the hell!" he growled. "Maybe you'd been better off not meeting me."

"What's wrong?"

He indicated the papers with a wave of one of his huge hands. "Aw, nuts! Oka's got the books all screwed up, half the bills aren't paid, there's no dough in the bank, and we got damned little coming from the account in San Francisco. And naturally, of course, Oka has to meet that sea gull of his and get plastered to the gills thirty minutes after he leaves the boat. All this mess to straighten out and he isn't even interested." He sucked in his breath sharply and paused for a minute. Then his eyes swept me up and down, suddenly conscious of the new clothes. "Well, well, quite an outfit. That's good gabardine. Maybe you got a few more bucks left in that wallet of yours?"

"Could be."

He leaned back against the wall and rubbed his fingers slowly over his chin, his eyes never leaving my face. When he had finished tabulating whatever was in his mind he said, "Let's put it on the table. How much do you have?"

"A little over eighteen hundred."

He was not at all surprised by the amount. He even seemed to expect it. He picked up a pencil and rapidly sketched off some figures on a piece of paper. Then he shoved the pencil aside, ran his tongue back and forth over his teeth, and squinted at me. "It could be done if you're willing. Sit down."

I pulled a bench around to the other side of the table and straddled it, facing him. "What do you have in mind?"

"Well, I guess you know Oka's all through. He's a boozer now. The only time he goes fishing is when he runs out of money. He'd rather stay ashore with that tramp of his."

"What is she like?"

Matt chuckled. "Can't you picture it, knowing him? Strictly a bum. But maybe we can help him get his wish and leave him ashore for good. I'm not bragging, Tom, but I know the fishing game inside out and now I know the shark end of it. I can run this outfit without Oka and a lot better. Interested?"

"I don't know. Explain it."

"Right." He crossed his muscular arms on the table and leaned toward me. "I can get Oka to drop out of the picture and turn the boat charter over to us. That's where your dough comes in. Oka can stay ashore and collect two shares for the use of his nets. He'll go for that, because with the nets always at work he'll do better than he's doing now and can drink himself silly. Now, I get two shares as fisherman and skipper, and you get two shares as fisherman and holder of the charter. The regular fishermen get a share each. That's nine shares. All expenses, maintenance, upkeep of the nets, and all that are deducted before any shares are paid out. That's the usual way it's done. Maybe we can make money."

"Is eighteen hundred enough?"

Matt shrugged. "Should be. If it isn't, we'll make it stretch." He raised his arms to lean his chin on his fists and looked into my eyes. "All right. How about it? Do you go for the deal, or does it smell worse than I think you smell to yourself?"

It was a crude way to express it, but he was so right that it hit me with the force of a physical blow.

I wondered how people learned to accept themselves without disgust. Some naturally went to psychiatrists. That was all right for people who needed a crutch, but it was not for me. I had no need to look behind mirrors. I was already well aware of part of the shadow behind the glass. The only thing left to do was bring it into focus. For that task I lacked a proper sense of perspective. You can't very well understand yourself, or anyone else, when you live on a mountain top. You must be able to walk in the valleys, I told myself.

That opportunity had never before presented itself but now it was mine to grasp. I was unknown, it was possible that I could continue hiding my identity and the biggest break had already been made. I could never possibly have arranged it in that fashion. It seemed as if the gods had simply placed it in my lap, perhaps to laugh about later. That I would never know—until later.

I balanced Matt's proposition against the thought of simply wandering in space and time until I should have to go back. Matt offered a sort of adventure, anonymity, facelessness, and the opportunity to gain perspective. It was a chance to learn how to live again. In spite of the accidental break, I was still faced with the death wish, perhaps now to a heightened degree. Worried and disgusted, wandering without roots and lost in space could be fatal. The law of averages catches up sooner or later, especially when the death wish is driving a man.

I remembered a lecture that Dr. Hughes had given

me the year before: "All people have the death wish in some degree, Howard, which is mainly why people do such reckless things, but you have it in every cell of your body. You're without an anchor. You lack stability. You drive a car beyond the limits of safety—which is reveling in the imminence of death—you enjoy flying in weather that has the airliners grounded and—now, don't stop me, I mean this—your furious pursuit of other men's wives is not a sexual drive at all but is really part and parcel of the death wish—arousing the killing wrath of the husband. One of these days that wish is going to be fulfilled. And I don't think it will take very long. No man can roll sevens at every shake of the dice."

Perhaps seven would not turn up again as it had the night of the accident. I had held the dice too long.

Matt interrupted my reverie by saying, "Well, I don't blame you if you don't think too much of the idea."

"It isn't that. I was thinking of something else." Then I remembered the statement I had made to Steve Moore, that I would see him in the sardine fleet, and realized that subconsciously I had already made up my mind. That made it easier to say, "Sure, I'll go along with you."

Matt grinned and reached over to squeeze my arm in a grip of steel. "Good boy. You won't regret it."

I wondered....

CHAPTER FIVE

Matt and I celebrated our possible partnership for a while that evening, but I was in no mood to get drunk so I returned to the hotel and retired early. I slept badly, however, tossing and turning all night, getting up every hour or so for a smoke or a drink and, when sleeping, dreaming of Bunny and the accident, and laughing at myself in the role of a fisherman. Toward morning I fell into a sounder, more refreshing sleep.

Ginny Norton awakened me on the telephone a little after ten. She wanted to return the twenty she had borrowed and said that she would drop by the hotel. I told her it was not necessary, but she insisted, so I gave her the room number.

She arrived a few minutes after I had shaved, soaked in a tub, (I didn't think I would ever rid myself of the smell of that galley) and dressed. When she knocked at the door I called to her to come in. I stood before the bureau mirror knotting a tie and watched her in the mirror as she came into the room. She was wearing a gay peasant outfit with a quilted skirt, a multi-colored sash, and an off-the-shoulders white blouse that accented the swelling of her breasts. She reminded me a little of Jane Russell, though darker and of a more sullen type. The bitter lines, too, were still etched about her full mouth, though she gave me a brief smile.

She was carrying a beach bag looped over her shoulder on a gold, knotted cord. She opened the bag, extracted a twenty-dollar bill, and crossed the room to place it before me on the bureau. Standing so close to me, I was able to inhale the exotic perfume she was wearing.

"Thanks for the loan, Tom. I hope it didn't put you out."

I finished knotting the tie and said, "Not at all." I got my coat out of the closet, slid it on and looked back at her. She was sitting on the edge of the bed, her legs crossed, lighting a cigarette. "But why all the rush?"

"Oh, I just wanted to get it back to you, and Matt told me where you were staying, so—" She shrugged, then swung her eyes slowly about to appraise the little room. "Strictly third-rate, isn't it? But no other fisherman from the *Rosita* could afford this room."

I stared at her with surprise. "At two-fifty a day?"

"Too much. Better save your money. You'll need it, now that you're going in with Matt."

"He told you?"

"Yes. I ran into him on Cannery Row a little while ago." She leaned back on an elbow and regarded me through half-narrowed eyes. "I know where you can get by more cheaply than this, a little cottage that rents for thirty a month."

I didn't know you could rent a dog kennel for that price but I said, "Sounds good."

"I know the old gal who owns it. Want me to ask her about it?"

"Yes. I would appreciate that." We fell into an awkward silence for a moment, then I thought of breakfast and asked if she would join me, but she had already eaten. "How about coming along for coffee?"

She was thoughtfully silent for a moment, then said, "I'm really on my way to the beach at Carmel. Would you like to go along?"

"Sure."

"Then I'll go with you for some coffee."

We left the room and went down the single flight of stairs to the main floor. As we were going through the tiny lobby, the clerk glanced at us from behind his desk and smirked at Ginny.

"Morning, Miss Norton."

She looked annoyed as she replied, "Good morning, Henry."

The silly smirk on his old face became deeper and somehow leering. "Lovely day, isn't it?"

"It was."

When we got out on the sidewalk she swore under her breath as she took my arm. "That," she said, slowly and bitterly, "is another nail in the coffin of my beautiful reputation. In case you don't know it, I've just spent the night with you."

"Oh, now wait—"

"Really. You see, he wasn't behind the desk when I came in. He didn't see me go upstairs. He only saw me come down. So, as far as he's concerned, I've been with you all night."

"Isn't that stretching circumstance a bit too far?"

"Not where I'm concerned."

"In that case, I'll straighten him out when I get back."

"Oh, don't be silly. He wouldn't believe a word you'd have to say. He's probably telling some of his old cronies about it right now. Give it a few days and everyone will be talking about my new lover."

"You're not really serious."

"But I am. I've been going through this for years. Don't give it a thought."

I remembered what Matt had had to say and could see how it would be. I glanced at the lush curves of her body swaying at my side and said aloud, "Yes, I can see how it is. You can hardly blame them, though."

Her eyelids flickered, whether in anger or amusement I couldn't tell.

We went into a coffee shop farther up the street and, after breakfast, around the corner to a Cadillac convertible parked against the curb. Ginny slid behind the wheel, pushed a button to run the top down, and looked inquiringly at me. I slid onto the seat at her side, slammed the door, and started to laugh.

"Yesterday," I said, "you were broke. Today you turn up with a Cadillac. Not bad."

She winked at me, started the engine and pulled away from the curb. "It belongs to the boss."

"Yesterday you didn't have a boss."

"I had one before the day was over. I go to work at the Las Olas bar this evening. About the car, it isn't what you're thinking, either."

"I'm not thinking."

"Martinelli, that's my boss, is an old friend of my father's. He has nine kids, at least five of them older than me. There is also a Mrs. Martinelli. Her English isn't very good, but she's one of the nicest persons I've ever known. In fact, I'm staying with them until I get a little ahead and find a place of my own. All your questions answered?"

"I didn't ask."

"You didn't have to. All a man has to do is look, and I know. Twenty-two years old and, believe me, I could give advice to a burleycue queen."

I had a hunch and said, "Adding or subtracting a few years?"

She slanted me a quick look from the corners of her eyes. The first warm smile I had seen tugged at the corners of her mouth as she turned her attention back to the traffic. "All right, Mr. Counsellor, I'm actually nineteen. But, for God's sake, keep that to yourself Or I won't be allowed to work in a bar."

"Your Mr. Martinelli must know."

"Oh, he does, but he doesn't mind. I have fake social security cards, driver's license, and everything else with the wrong age on them. Have had for years."

That gave me an idea which I sat back to think about. I would need such fake identification, too. If anyone ever got a look at the wallet in my pocket my little masquerade would go up in smoke.

She seemed to enjoy talking to me and chattered away in her soft, throaty voice as we went up the long hill out of Monterey and toward Carmel, four miles away. Her conversation skipped from subject to subject, and although she was not really trying to tell me about herself, I did learn a lot about her. Obviously, poverty had always been another member of her family, even in good times. Her father had evidently been a bad fisherman and an indifferent provider at all times. She and her mother had had to scrape by on virtually next to nothing. She knew what it was like to eat seven varieties of fish seven days a week, and hated any food that came out of the sea.

She had matured at an unusually early age, so much so that she had no friends of her own age and school was torture for her. Little boys, on the other hand, had swarmed about her, and she remembered them as dirty, loathsome little creatures. Matters changed when she went into high school, where most of the other girls were also matured, but not for the better. The older boys gathered about her in such numbers and dogged her footsteps so constantly that they erected a barrier toward any friendships she may have had with the other girls. She was the most dated girl in the school—and probably the loneliest.

She entered and won her first beauty contest at sixteen and quit high school for a stenographer's job. She was not a very good stenographer, but none of her many bosses seemed to care. They were more interested in her. So she moved on from job to job and at last had found one that paid more than the others, that of a cocktail waitress.

"The salary isn't really very good," she explained, "but that isn't important. Men always overtip a good-looking waitress, especially if they've been drinking. Anywhere else I couldn't do better than fifty a week. In a bar I average over a hundred a week."

"Not bad."

"Of course," she said, "you hear a lot of rough talk and you run into a lot of abuse, but you learn how to handle it. Other customers, too, are quick to protect you if things start getting out of hand."

"Saloon gallantry."

"I guess."

She continued talking as we went down the other side of the hill and turned onto Ocean Avenue, which led down into the picturesque village of Carmel. I had not been there in a few years and, as we proceeded down the street divided by shrubbery and trees, looked with interest at the new shops and the new construction going on. In spite of the additions, however, Carmel still retained an atmosphere of peace and serenity and a total lack of bustle. It was fast becoming a major tourist center yet it remained the quaint village under the trees.

We parked at the foot of Ocean Avenue, left the car and walked down the steeply sloping sand bank to the beach. For a change, there was no breeze blowing, the air was warm and languid, and the restless sea was murmurously quiet. The long, wide beach stretched along the bay in an arc to our right and left, probably the whitest sand in the world. Back in the dunes and along the edge of Scenic Drive were the famed Monterey cypress trees, gnarled and twisted into weird shapes by the wind and ocean storms.

We selected a spot on the beach, back against the bank, in a protected little cove filled with sun and with some privacy. I had no trunks, so I took off my jacket and shirt and stripped to the waist. I stretched out on my back, cupped my head in my hands to keep my hair out of the sand, and looked up to watch Ginny. She kicked her sandals free, lifted the blouse over her head, pulled the zipper of her skirt, and stepped out of that. I could see what Matt had meant about Ginny's liking to swim in the nude. What emerged was almost that; virtual nudity. It was fortunate that we did have some privacy in our little cove. Her full breasts were scantily covered by the flimsiest of halters and the scrap of polka-dotted material she wore about her hips could practically have been placed in a thimble. I have seen such Bikini outfits in pinup pictures, but never before on a beach. With her narrow waist, generous hips and breasts, and creamy skin she looked more nude than if she had actually been.

She seemed not to give it a thought, however, but took a towel from her beach bag and stretched out on it at my side. She sighed and said, "I love the sun."

"I imagine you would get badly sunburned, with that fair skin."

"Peculiarly, I don't. A little pinkish sometimes, but that's all. And I never tan." She shielded her eyes to glance at my chest. "But you have a good tan already."

"Summers I get dark as a Kanaka."

"That, too, you know, is not the mark of a fisherman, or anyone who works on boats. They always wear something. Only their faces burn to leather."

"I've never said I was a fisherman. Matt's going to be my instructor."

"I know."

She was going to start questioning me, so I said, "Tell me about your cousin, Gail. You two aren't a bit alike. Distant cousins?"

"No." I was watching her and saw her bite her lower lip before she continued. "Our fathers were brothers. Mine was impractical, kind of an idealist. He loved the sea. Gail's father was the businessman of the two. He fished for a while, I've heard—neither had much schooling—but he got a job in a cannery as soon as he could. He worked his way up to manager, saved his money, and went into business on his own. He made a success of it. The Norton Cannery is the biggest on the Row."

"But not doing so well?"

"Not since he died. Gail doesn't know the business, the managers are a bunch of thieves, and, besides, the seasons have been bad for everyone." She shielded her eyes again and gave me another quick glance. "You've met her, I take it?"

"Twice."

"Oh."

"What do you mean by that?"

"Nothing. Beautiful, isn't she?"

"Mmmm, yes. She is a beautiful woman. Older than you?"

"Four years."

I turned onto an elbow so that I could watch her expression. That was a mistake. I could hardly take my eyes from her body. "I have a hunch you two aren't particularly close friends."

"Well, we don't hate each other, but there's no love lost, either. Gail was raised differently. They always had money, she went to good schools, took ballet and music and riding and things like that." She laughed throatily as she said, "Gail was brought up to be a lady and, by God, she lets you know it."

"I didn't have that impression."

"You're a man, that's why. There's something about her—something with all men, regardless of who they are—"

I suggested, "You mean she is constantly seeking their approval?"

"That's it. So you saw that. Well! But with women she's a dirty, little snob. And with me—my God! She'd rather I'd go lose myself somewhere. She's afraid my reputation is rubbing off on her. She's scared to death to be seen in my company. You know something? We haven't spent ten minutes together in the last three or four years. To hell with her."

I smiled down at her and said, "You know something yourself—you're a very frank person with me. Why is that?"

She looked up into my eyes with a frown and was thoughtfully silent for some time. At last she said, "I don't know. I've wondered, too. I suppose it's because you're kind of a unique character."

"In what way?"

"That's even harder to say. You're kind of a gentleman, some ways, you're not nervy like most men I run into, you seem to have better sense than most, and yet—well, there's a feeling of danger, too, something wrong about you. It's funny, though, but I feel safe with you. Relaxed. You know?"

"You're quite a character analyst. But I hope you don't take me for a eunuch incapable of making a play for you. If you could read my mind right now you might not feel so relaxed."

She shook her dark head and smiled faintly. "That isn't what I mean. You could make a play, all right, but it isn't something I'd have to worry about."

"Why not?"

"Like I say, I've been up against all types. Where a

woman's concerned, you're not the rough, shoving, aggressive type. You're too smooth for that. You take your time and give warning. Besides, you're conceited. A woman has to meet you at least halfway or you lose interest. Right?"

"Well—" I stopped and laughed.

"So I feel safe with you. You see?"

I rolled over to my back and closed my eyes against the glare of the sun. In a moment I was asleep. I suppose I slept twenty or thirty minutes; I awakened with my face and chest bathed in perspiration. Ginny was propped on an elbow, leaning partly over me, intently studying my face. The position of her shoulder had loosened the halter over her right breast. I looked up into her eyes and slowly raised a hand until my fingers were at the back of her neck. I pulled her down until her soft lips were pressed against mine and started to put an arm about her waist, but suddenly she gasped and pulled away from me.

"Oh, no. No!"

I sat up and stared at her. "What's the matter with you?"

Her face went hard and almost coarse as she snapped, "Never a fisherman!"

"What are you talking about? You know damned well I haven't been a fisherman."

"But you are now. You're going in with Matt, aren't you?"

"So?"

"So from now on, as far as I'm concerned, you have the plague." She got quickly to her feet and reached for her clothes. "We'd better get back to town."

I looked up at her and had to smile. She represented quite a challenge.

CHAPTER SIX

Getting Oka Halversen to retire as skipper of the *Rosita* was not as simple as Matt had anticipated. One difficulty was that he was already on a binge and his alcohol-soaked brain could not understand logic. Another was that his girlfriend, Mabel, was suspicious of Matt's motives. She was the kind Navy men call sea gulls, a frowzy, beer-blown woman who had never seen better days and never would. Her life had started at the grave.

But Oka himself was the biggest stumbling block. He had followed the sea too long to retire so suddenly and live off the shares afforded him by the use of his nets. The sea was in his blood. It was seemingly impossible to convince him that he was no longer operating in an efficient manner and that he would do better for himself by staying ashore and keeping the boat at work as much as possible. Oka was tempted, but he would not let go.

I took matters in my own hands after a few days, when I saw that Matt was getting nowhere. I had found the San Diego address of Mrs. Halversen in the cabin of the *Rosita*, so I closed the door to whatever conscience I may have had and composed a letter to her. I signed it "A Friend," after informing her that her husband was carrying on with another woman and that I, "a God-fearing person," thought that she should know about it before it became a scandal in Monterey.

That letter did the trick. It was sent special delivery airmail, and brought Mrs. Halversen storming into Monterey on practically the next plane. What transpired between them I got secondhand from Matt. He met me in my hotel room, an anxious frown creasing his brows, and explained that Mrs. Halversen was in town and raising all kinds of hell.

He watched me sharply as he said, "I can't figure it out. Oka has been carrying on with this tramp a couple of years and nothing has happened before. No one he knows would be interested in causing this to happen. But now, just when we need him on a spot, there he is, all set up for us. Odd coincidence, don't you think?" He went into the bathroom, got the water glass, and came back to pour some whisky into it. He threw his head back, washed the whisky down his throat in one gulp, then looked suspiciously at me, his narrowed blue eyes like hard agates. "You wouldn't know anything about it, would you?" He waited.

I said blandly, "I don't even know the woman."

"Yeah. Well, she caught Oka with Mabel so they're breaking up."

"Oka and Mabel?"

"Oka and his wife. She says she's going to get a divorce and I believe her. She learned for the first time, too, that Oka's a boozer. That hit her just as hard as finding out about Mabel. You know how these old-country wives are, especially the Scandinavians."

"How is Oka taking it?"

"Pretty hard. It's like the sea. He's been married to

her too long. Divorce is the end of the world. He's stunned." Matt sighed and said, "However, it's working out well for us. The skipper is too concerned with his own affairs to even think about fishing. He told me to go ahead with whatever we wish to do. Two shares for the use of his nets will satisfy him."

"Then it's all set?"

"Yes. You can go with me tomorrow while we switch the boat charter to your name. Then we go fishing." He squinted at me again, ice-cold lights in the depths of his eyes. "This is a dirty, raw deal, Tom. Very dirty. Any man who would cause a thing like this to happen is lower than a slimy eel. Do you know what that is?"

"No."

"When sharks are helpless in the nets slimy eels go through them like a dose of salts and clean out their guts. The shark is no longer good for anything."

He leaned back against the wall and puffed at a cigarette, his eyes fastened on mine. Evidently he discovered nothing there because after a few moments he began to relax. But I had discovered something. I was coming into focus, through Matt's eyes. What I had caused to happen had been done without compunction, even without emotion. Oka had been in the way. I had removed him. There was no more to it than that. But, according to Matt, that had been the wrong thing to do. So I was a slimy eel that had just gutted a man. But perhaps, in spite of his size, Matt belonged to the jellyfish family. It would be interesting to find out who was in what school.

With Oka out of the way the change of charter was accomplished without difficulty and the *Rosita* was readied for sea. I thought that was simply a matter of putting food aboard, starting the engine, and casting off. I could not have been more wrong. All of us worked from dawn to dusk and worked hard. I worked harder than the others since it was all new to me. Mending the nets was the toughest job. They had been at sea for many months and needed a thorough overhauling. My hands were soon covered with blisters and every night I had nightmares about those nets. A dozen times a day I was ready to quit, but I kept going. It was not pride that kept me at it. Gail Norton was mainly responsible.

She came down the wharf at least twice a day to call on Matt and, I was convinced, to watch me. She never talked with me, except for a cool "Hello" and a very rare "Nice day, isn't it?" In fact, we had never really spoken to each other except for the two occasions of our first meeting and the time I had run into her with Steve Moore. But whenever I glanced suddenly at her—she was usually seated in the shade where she could watch all of us at the nets—more often than not I found her eyes turned on me. I had a feeling that she was taking strange delight in my obvious suffering. It was plain to her, or anyone, that I was not a fisherman, yet, I was sure, it annoyed her that she could not place me against any other background. She was the kind of woman who had to file a man neatly in place and forevermore keep him there. It infuriated her that she could not do that with me. Possibly, too, the fact that I had dismissed her so abruptly when she had escorted me to the hotel was still a source of annoyance to her. She didn't know whether she had my approval or not. So she enjoyed watching me sweat over the nets and salve the blisters on my hands, and she waited for me to quit. Perhaps I would have if she had not been there. With her present it was impossible. I had to keep at it.

On the other hand, her presence was even more disturbing than she realized. She was a constant reminder that, in a way, I was being a damned fool. Working in filthy clothes, fouled with creosote, my ears constantly assailed with the ignorant chatter of the rest of the crew, I had only to glance at her cool poise, sophisticated makeup, and expensive dress to be projected back into the atmosphere where I belonged. She was too much like my own kind. I almost hated her for it.

The day before we were due to sail, she told Matt that she would like to give him two cases of Heineken's beer to take along. He was too busy to collect them so he asked me to go with her to pick them up. I had a hunch that she had timed it in such a manner that I would be the one to go with her. I surprised a tiny smile in her eyes and was positive of it.

We went down the wharf to her car, parked in the lot by the old customs building. It was a Lincoln sedan, about three years old, in immaculate condition. I was in dirty clothes, so she threw a cover over the seat I was to sit on. But, even so, the fishy smell of my clothes permeated the car and we had to open the windows. I derived some sort of perverse pleasure in stinking up that car.

She lived on what is known as the Mesa, above Fremont and between Monterey and the college. Most of the homes there were estates of a few acres, usually with thick cypress hedges for privacy and chalk-rock walls smothered with rose bushes and vines. A half-circular driveway curved in before her home, a rambling, early California-Monterey construction of possibly twelve or more rooms and three-foot-thick adobe walls. It was a decidedly gracious home and beautifully proportioned.

While opening the door, Gail explained, "The house was built in the eighteen hundreds, then renovated a couple of times before my father bought it. He also had most of it rebuilt, except for the walls and the floors." As we stepped into the cool entrance hallway she directed my attention to the floors. "It's all hand-adzed oak, three inches thick. It would cost a fortune to duplicate today."

She made me realize at once that almost everything about the place would cost a fortune to duplicate. She was not too far wrong, at that, though our individual ideas of what constituted a fortune were probably far apart. The ceiling beams in the long living room were huge oak timbers that had come out of an early sailing vessel and the baseboards were of teak that had been brought around the Horn. A good proportion of the furniture was early American, as I had expected, some of it even museum pieces, but it was nicely balanced with enormous couches, modern paintings, thick rugs with colorful patterns, and light draperies that lessened the somber feeling of the thick walls. The only thing not quite in the best of taste was a too lavish display of silver candelabras. The effect would have been better if a few of the pieces had been removed.

She asked me to wait in the library and disappeared in the direction of the kitchen. She returned after a few moments with a silver tray, unnecessarily large, carrying two glasses of foaming beer. She glanced nervously at my dirty clothes and was worried about where I was going to sit. I was tempted to pick the best chair in the room but leaned against the fireplace mantel instead. She heaved a little sigh of relief, then draped herself gracefully on a leather couch across the room.

Her nervousness remained, however, though for a different reason. She was obviously going out of her way to impress me and was anxious to know my reaction to the house as a backdrop for Gail Norton. It was apparent that she felt I was properly overwhelmed, but she would remain anxious until I actually put it into words. The approval she was always seeking had to be oral. I asked her, "Do you live here all alone?"

"Yes." She flushed a bit as she said, "A maid comes in part-time and there is also a part-time man to take care of the gardens." She felt the need to explain and gave me a patronizing smile as she said quickly, "I don't like servants about all the time. They get underfoot, you know."

"And they're also expensive."

The smile faded and her eyes slid away from mine. She took a long swallow of beer to cover her confusion, then said brightly, "Yes, they are, aren't they? It's really a problem today. But I don't suppose you would lose any sleep over it."

I thought of the staff of eight in my Bel-Air home and said, "Not at all. But I would imagine a house of this size would require more help. Why do you live in it?"

"I beg your pardon!"

"It's too big for one person and I've heard you can't afford it. So why don't you sell? You could probably get a good price for it."

She gasped, "Well, of all the impertinence—"

"Look, you brought me here for one reason, so that you could patronize me and impress me. I don't impress easily."

"I suppose," she snapped angrily, "you're used to so much better. You let me tell you something, Mr. Howie. Matt has told me all about you. When he picked you up, you were just a drunken bum. You're no fisherman, but he figures you're some kind of drifter, a sort of—well—"

"Go ahead. A sort of what?"

"Well, some sort of parasite. He says your knowledge of boats comes from yachts more than any other kind."

"He's smarter than I realized."

"So he figures you've been hanging around wealthy people—"

"The boy's a born analyst."

"As a kind of stooge, or something of that sort. So I don't see where you get off telling other people what to do."

"I wasn't. I was just making a sensible observation. The fact still remains that the house is too big for you. Tell me truthfully—do you really enjoy living here all alone?"

She tried to hang onto her anger, but it dissipated. She sat back in the couch looking a bit tired and just a little forlorn. Her pose of crisp sophistication was gone, at least for the moment.

"No," she admitted. "It's really lonely here. But I would rather die than lose—I mean, sell this house."

I sipped at my beer, then said, "It means something more to you than just a home. It's a symbol."

"Yes."

"Of defiance?"

She looked across at me, her eyes wide and startled. "Why do you say that?"

"Probably because it's true. I've learned a lot about you, particularly, the situation with your cannery. You're just about broke and on the verge of going down the drain. You feel that most people are smugly waiting for that to happen and probably enjoying it. So you're hanging on as hard as you can to all the possessions that, in your mind, place you on a level above them. Once you begin to lose things, especially this house, it will break you."

She shuddered, closed her eyes, and nodded. "Yes. You don't know what it's like. It's a nightmare. People are always so gleeful when someone is having a bad time of it, particularly a person they've had to look up to. I hate them," she cried. "I hate them all. Jackals. Snapping little terriers." She opened her eyes again and stared at me, her words coming forth in a furious rush. "But they aren't going to have the satisfaction of watching me crash. I won't allow it to happen. The cannery is still there and it's still the biggest on the Row. The equipment is there. Everything is there. Just one good pilchard season and I'll have the last laugh on all of them."

"Or," I suggested, "a change of management?"

"I don't understand—"

"Steve Moore."

She looked away from me, her earlier nervousness returning. "People certainly gossip, don't they? And you—you're more presumptuous than anyone I've ever known. I don't know that I like it."

"Of course you don't like it. You don't like a lot of things about me. I'm just a drifter, a stooge, trying to learn the fishing game. You're a decidedly beautiful woman. So you don't understand why I don't fall flat on my face and kiss your big toe. Would it be too much of a shock if I told you that I've known all kinds of beautiful women?"

She stared at the bandage on my forehead and the dirty adhesive tape across my nose and the filthy clothes I was wearing and burst into a musical laugh. I laughed with her, though for another reason.

I finished my beer, placed it on the mantel, and told her, "Let's get the beer for Matt."

We went out to the kitchen, and I carried the two cases out the back way and around to the car. We returned to town in silence and went to the wharf. The guard gave us permission to go through, so Gail drove down the wharf and parked just above the *Rosita*. I put the beer out on the wharf and called to Matt. He came out on deck and reached up for the cases as I handed them down to him.

When he carried them into the cabin, I turned back to the car and leaned in through the open window.

Gail was watching me curiously, the puzzled look in her eyes deeper than ever.

"Was that right?" she asked. "I mean what Matt had to say about you."

"Partly."

"I can see what he means, some ways. You're a maddeningly indifferent person, almost as if you had great heaps of money yourself."

"Is there a certain attitude that goes with great wealth?"

"Oh, definitely. It's odd, but you have it." She smiled and added, "Some of it must have rubbed off on you. Your rudeness, for example." Then she laughed and leaned across the seat to place a hand on my arm. "I'm sorry, Tom. I'm being the rude one. I don't know why, but there is something about you that aggravates me. Will you forgive me?"

"Easily. If you'll have dinner with me when I come back."

Evidently she took that as my first indication of approval, for she smiled warmly at me. "Maybe," she said. "We'll see."

I stepped back from the car and watched her as she left. She took her time turning the car about, knowing that I was watching her. When she was finally straightened away, she gave me a friendly wave and rolled down the wharf. I turned around and saw Matt watching the little scene from the bridge of the *Rosita*. There was no approval in his eyes. He was scowling darkly and staring at me with an expression of anger. I stared back at him for a moment, then dropped down to the deck of the *Rosita*. When he joined me he had nothing to say, so I put the incident out of my mind.

There was little for me to do on the boat that evening, so after dinner I walked up to the cocktail room of the Las Olas Hotel, where Ginny was working. It was a large frame building built around a central open patio which could be seen from the bar or dining room. The barroom was fairly large, but the bar itself was small, with only a dozen stools and all of them occupied. I sat in a corner away from the bar, in a green leather chair at a tiny, round glass table. The atmosphere of the place was charming and rather quaint. The bar was also very popular.

It was about ten in the evening. Ginny worked from five to midnight, so she was on duty. I had expected to see her in some kind of uniform, but she wore, instead, a thin white blouse that accented her breasts, a gold stitched belt, and a pleated skirt that followed every line of her body as she walked. I noticed that the eyes of every man in the room followed her furtively as she moved about.

When she came to the table at which I was seated, she seemed surprised to see me. I asked her why. "Well," she replied, "this is a little off the beaten track for the average fisherman. The Las Olas is expensive."

I looked about the dimly lit room at the average-looking women and the men in their ready-made business suits. It seemed ordinary enough to me.

I ordered a highball from Ginny, then sat back to watch her at work. She was clever and she was unscrupulous. When she served mixed couples at a table she was quick and efficient. She knew better than to hover about and let her figure antagonize the women. But when she served men only she smiled brightly and warmly, was friendly with her conversation, and returned their good-natured banter with ribbing they enjoyed. Also, when she placed their glasses on the tables she leaned over a bit farther than was absolutely necessary, so that the thin blouse pulled tightly about her full breasts. Without exception, her tray always held a tip that was double what it would have been for anyone else. She knew every angle.

When she brought me another highball she also placed on the table a slip of paper on which was written a name and address. "That's the cottage I was telling you about, and the name of the woman who owns it. It's not occupied right now, so you might drop over and see it."

"Thanks. I will, as soon as we get back from fishing." I glanced about the room, then back at Ginny, who was standing there looking down at me. "You know, you're quite an artist. Do you enjoy this work?"

She shrugged a shoulder and replied coolly, "Not particularly. But I make more money at it than you will fishing."

She seemed so damnably self-sufficient that it began to get under my skin. I asked her, "Is that what counts?"

"I can't think of a better reason for working here."

"But a waitress—there isn't much prestige attached to that kind of job. Rather far down on the social scale. I should imagine you would try for something of more importance, where you meet a better class of people—"

"In a bar," she interrupted, an edge to her voice, "you

meet every class, even sea-going cooks."

"True enough. But you're their menial."

Her face flushed and her teeth closed whitely over her lower lip. It was apparently a point that disturbed her. That pleased me.

"For example," I said, "I would like a pack of matches."

She left me without hesitation and returned a moment later with some matches. She struck one of them and leaned over to light my cigarette, her dark eyes narrowly watching my expression. I inhaled, blew the smoke to the ceiling, then looked into her eyes.

"Also," I said, "I don't like this highball. Take it back and bring me another with less ice."

Her white cheeks flushed a deeper and more dangerous pink. "There is nothing wrong with the one you have."

"I am willing to pay for another. Go get it for me—if you don't mind."

"But the one you have—"

"Shall I ask the manager to get it for me? After all, I am not refusing to pay. Less ice, please."

She went to the bar and ordered another highball. When she brought it to me her eyes were glowing dangerously with frustration and rage.

Between clenched teeth, she asked, "Anything else— sir?"

"I'll call you if I need anything."

She left me as abruptly as if I had the plague and went to stand at the end of the bar. She was so exasperated that she was close to tears, blinking her eyes rapidly to hold them back. For a while the other customers had difficulty getting her attention.

Steve Moore entered the bar, slapped some of the men on the back, said "Hello" to practically everyone in the room, and took a just-vacated stool at the end of the bar next to Ginny's station. He was in a hearty, expansive mood and ordered a dozen or more drinks for people he knew. His heartiness faded as Ginny leaned over to whisper in his ear. His red face became even redder, if possible, and he twisted about on the stool to look in my direction. He remembered me and was not at all happy to see me. I smiled broadly and raised my glass toward him in a mock salute. He stared at me a moment longer, then turned away.

I finished my drink and called loudly, "Waitress!"

She tried to ignore me, but I called her again, a bit louder. People at the bar turned around to stare at me, so I called out, "Oh, girlie." The bartender frowned at Ginny and nodded his head in my direction. She snatched her tray from the bar and stalked to my table, her whole body quivering with tension.

"Another one, please. And don't forget, less ice. It's such a little thing to remember."

She brought the drink and stood before the table, waiting for me to pay her. I let her stand there and sipped slowly at the drink. When I saw that she was about to whirl away I took a twenty-dollar bill from my wallet and placed it on the tray. She sucked in her breath sharply and made change with shaking fingers. I picked up the money and put a ten-cent tip on the tray. Again she turned to leave.

I said quickly, "This table is a bit damp. Moisture from the glasses, you know. If you don't mind—?"

She stalked to the bar and returned with a damp bar cloth. She leaned over the table and industriously wiped it clean. Then her eyes came up and met mine so suddenly that I was not able to hide the smile in time. Her eyes flew open wide and the next thing I knew the wet bar cloth slapped viciously across my face.

It was almost as if a bomb had exploded. Customers kicked back their chairs, the bartender hurried to rush around the end of the bar, and Steve Moore came toward me like a football tackle, bellowing with rage. All of them got in each other's way, or I would have been severely mauled. As it was, I managed to exchange a few punches with Moore and some of the others, almost got my eyes scratched by Ginny, who was getting pretty hysterical, and was given the old bum's rush out of the bar.

Moore stood in the open door and yelled at me, "I'm giving you twenty-four hours to get out of town or, by God, you'll regret it. You hear me, you jerk?"

I sat on the sidewalk and looked back at him and thought that with a single phone call to Los Angeles, if I dared make it, I could smash his career in even less time than that. But then, as the door was slammed, I started to laugh. I was laughing so hard I had difficulty getting to my feet.

In my newly acquired bottom-level status, Ginny and Gail each represented an incomparable challenge. But the perversity of my nature was such that I had gone far out of my way to make them thoroughly dislike me. As Carleton, of course, I would have been catalogued as being rather quaintly eccentric, perhaps even entertaining. But Tom Howie, fisherman-cook, was an altogether different matter.

Yet, I realized, the challenge was now even greater than ever. If either of them could accept me as plain, ordinary Tom Howie it would be a remarkable achievement. I would learn more about myself in that direction than in any other. There are no mirrors quite as clear as a woman's eyes when there is apparently nothing to be gained.

I brushed off my clothes and walked down the street feeling oddly elated. Monterey was definitely offering a new interest in life.

CHAPTER SEVEN

It was an all-night run down the coast to the Disney-like rock of the Big Sur Coast Guard light station, where we put out the five sharks-gill nets, each about 2,400 feet long. The nets were ten-inch mesh, or five inches square to the mesh, and twenty squares wide, which made them a little over eight feet in width. They were put out with long identification poles, red flags tied on the tips, anchors to hold them down, and bobbing floats at each end. One side of the nets was loaded with lead weights and the other with small, round floats wrapped in netting. Matt had them put down in about forty-two fathoms of water and scattered over a wide area a few miles offshore.

I helped Tony and Pete with the nets, running them aft over the spreaders, and also did the cooking. As soon as the nets were out we had to run for the lee of the Big Sur rock, while a storm blew along the coast. Matt explained that ordinarily we would have returned to Monterey and waited two or three days before going back to the nets, but he wouldn't chance it in the storm. *Rosita* was a round-bottom boat with a vicious roll. Like most purse seiners of any size, she was not a good heavy-weather boat.

We remained in the lee of the rock until the storm blew out three days later, then returned to the nets. That was when the really hard work started. What had gone before had been play. Getting in those nets was the most back-breaking labor I have ever experienced.

The long pole was taken aboard first, then the line was run in over runners on the starboard side and around a power winch padded with old rubber tires for a better grip. The winch was then started until the first anchor came up. The anchor was stowed on one of the thwarts and the line coiled, then the line kept coming up from the sea until the net itself came out of the water and started aboard through the runners.

As the net comes out of the water and goes around the winch it is all squeezed together. One man stands at the starboard side to watch the net come out of the sea and handle the winch clutch so that not too much strain is placed on it. Another stands by the main hatch cover aft of the winch to keep the net from getting tangled. That was my job. Two other men stand in the sternway, one on each side, and separate the net and spread it out and fold it so that it is ready to go back in the sea again.

When a shark comes out of the sea, caught in the net, the winchman gaffs it, runs it around the winch, then throws in the clutch when the fish is over the hatch. He and I then untangle the fish from the net, a rough job, slide it off the hatch to the deck, and start the winch again to bring in more net. It takes about an hour and a half to bring in each net, unload the fish, then run the anchors, floats, and net back into the sea again over the aft spreaders.

We started with the nets at five in the morning and finished shortly after noon. I was exhausted, but managed to stagger into the galley and fix some sandwiches for lunch, which we washed down with cold beer or red wine. Then I went aft again, as Matt headed the *Rosita* for Monterey, and helped clean the fish. Tony took over the wheel while Matt came aft and directed our labors.

We had a number of halibut and various other fish, but the main haul was a hundred and twenty-six soup-fin sharks. We cleaned out the livers, putting the male and female in separate cans, except that the livers from females carrying pups went into the male cans. That cleaning job was a bloody mess and soon had the deck looking like the floor of a slaughter house. Johnson hosed it off, and the job was done just as we were rounding Cypress Point off the Monterey Peninsula. Matt looked the cans over with a broad, satisfied grin. According to his rough estimate, we had something better than two-thousand-dollars' worth of liver loaded with vitamin A. Even after the expenses of the boat were deducted, that meant over two hundred dollars per share.

Johnson and Pete pounded me on the back and claimed that I had brought them luck. Even Tony, at least for the moment, lost his smoldering resentment toward me. We broke out the last case of beer and celebrated. It was curious how that small triumph gave me such a warm, inner glow and a feeling of great accomplishment.

I turned back time but a few short months and remembered how a new oil field had gone. My agents had acquired some Wilmington property lying between two faults that had never proven out well, even in low gravity. But the Carleton petroleum engineers had a hunch that there was a high-gravity dome much deeper down. They sold me on the hunch, so I told them to gamble on it, figuring to lose perhaps a hundred or two hundred thousand on the deal. The first well, however, came in with a capacity of eight hundred barrels a day, fell off a bit, then steadied at seven hundred a day. Other wells were started at once and what should have been a losing gamble turned into an income of better than a half million dollars a year.

Everyone in the petroleum business applauded my daring and "great vision" and I even became a little smug about it. Yet that venture was nothing and paled into insignificance alongside the way I felt about catching some fish and earning a few hundred dollars strictly with the muscles of my back and arms.

Matt and I relaxed on the stern, basking in the warm sun and drinking beer as we rounded Point Pinos and started into Monterey Bay. The big man was feeling good and predicted that now, with Oka out of the way, we would do some real fishing and clean up.

He slapped my back and said, "If this keeps up, I may even be able to get back in sardines this coming season. And if that works out all right I may even try to get married—again."

"What do you mean by that?"

"Well, so far, she won't have me."

I felt a cold chill travel up my spine. "Not Gail Norton."

"Of course."

"There is one completely selfish and self-centered woman."

I thought he would take exception to that, but he chuckled and said, "Who isn't? Look, I'm not out here to make money for you and the rest of the crew. Personally, I don't give a damn what happens to any of you. I'm here to make it for myself and I'd cut your throat if you got in the way. So I don't blame Gail for the way she is. Besides, you don't know her."

"But maybe I do."

Matt chuckled again, a hollow rumble deep in his barrel chest. "No, you don't. You're a fairly shrewd character, some ways, and I notice you size people up pretty well, but you could go completely haywire where Gail is concerned. You have to look behind that glittering surface she wears to find the woman. There's a lot there."

He still had his hand on my back and absent-mindedly started scratching it. "You listen to me, Tom. You've been around town, now, long enough to learn something about the Nortons. I can tell you more.

Every young squirt I know, including me, was after the two of them. Hell, we used to follow them around town like a pack of hound dogs. They were always outstanding gals, though in different ways. Gail was always the one who appealed to me. I guess I've been nuts about her for years. But she'd have no part of me. She has always liked me, I know, but that's as far as it goes. Her sights are on bigger game." He paused, then sighed and added, "She was raised that way, you see."

"And you don't mind?"

He dropped his hand from my back to light a cigarette and shrugged. "What the hell's the difference? Does the price matter when you really want something?"

"Yes, but—" then I fell silent.

All my life I had been worried about women wanting to marry me solely because of the Carleton fortune. That worry had not been a vain one. It was all too true. It was so true that it had been impossible for me to differentiate between a woman on the prowl and another who may have been sincerely interested in me as a person. In fact, I doubted, was even rather positive, that no woman had ever been in love with me or even close to it.

Matt did not have that worry. I would have thought he was in the ideal position for choosing a wife. He had nothing to offer but himself. That should have been enough, however, considering his size, his rugged good looks, his fairly even disposition, the fact that he was a good worker and anxious to get ahead, and that, no matter how you looked at him, he was strictly all man in every way. Yet he wished to acquire a fortune, too, even though a modest one, to attract the one woman in whom he was interested. That he should have been sufficient in himself was not important to him. He was willing to take second place to Gail's desires. There was nothing meek or mild about his spirit, so I could only conclude he was very much in love. It was a topsy-turvy situation.

I was beginning to feel something approaching real affection for Matt, so when we landed I went in search of Gail to reappraise her. I learned, however, that she had run up to San Francisco, probably in the endeavor to raise money for her cannery. I didn't see her again for a number of weeks.

We were kept busy fishing off Big Sur, tanning and mending nets, working on *Rosita's* cranky diesel, and sending off cans of shark livers. The haul continued good and hit an occasional peak of four or five thousand dollars a trip: The crew blossomed out in new clothes and second-hand automobiles and their morale soared high. There was never any more grumbling aboard ship and they obeyed Matt's orders cheerfully. It was a far different crew from the one I had joined originally and, though it was all due to getting rid of Oka and Matt taking charge, the men nevertheless felt that I was partly responsible, too, and held a friendly attitude toward me.

I heard, however, that Steve Moore was asking questions concerning my identity and hinting that possibly I had a jail record. His warning for me to get out of town in twenty-four hours could obviously not be put into execution, so he was trying other tactics.

His attitude was childlike, but there was tremendous danger in it for me. Any real investigation would easily unearth my identity. I thought of appeasing him in some way or other, but knew that could not be done. His dislike for me was too intense. Then, too, any change in my own attitude toward him would be a clear indication that I was frightened and would arouse the suspicions of everyone around me. We had selected each other as antagonists and I had to keep it that way, in spite of the dangers involved.

The only sensible thing to do was to build up a phony background for myself and establish the name of Tom Howie so well that not even Moore would bother to pry into my past. So I went out of my way to acquire credentials identifying Tom Howie, fisherman. It was actually an easy matter. I got a social security card in that name, joined the fishermen's union, took out a membership in a book club, established a certain small credit rating in the shops about town, and acquired identification cards that seemingly went into the past. Then I bought a small coupé and got a driver's license. The latter presented a difficulty, as California law requires a thumbprint on the license. I deliberately smudged the print, then a second and a third. The harassed official behind the counter lost patience and let the last smudge go by. I was then fully equipped for identification.

I also moved from the small hotel and took the cottage Ginny had recommended. It had a kitchen, living room, and bedroom, with a pint-sized bathroom too small for a tub but with an adequate shower. A small, white frame building, it sat at the rear of a sloping lot not far from Monterey's Colton Hall. The cottage could hardly be seen from the street, as the forward part of the lot was filled with wild ivy, ferns, and a number of pine trees. The landlady explained that it was originally meant to be a guest house, but that the main structure had never been built. The privacy it enjoyed by virtue of the natural green screening was excellent. The place was about half the size of my gatekeeper's cottage on the Carleton estate, but I rather enjoyed it, undoubtedly because I was paying for it with the labor of my own hands.

It was, however, sparsely and cheaply furnished, so I bought a comfortable leather chair and couch for the living room, a number of sporting prints for the walls, and a studio-type bed with a sponge-rubber mattress. Another addition was a portable, reed-covered bar, which I placed in a corner of the living room. But the new furnishings made the shabby draperies and curtains look worse than ever, so I went shopping for new ones.

A small shop on Alvarado Street made up some white, glass-cloth draperies for the living room and checked gingham curtains for the kitchen. I went in to collect them late one afternoon and was coming out of the shop with the bundles when I ran into Ginny Norton. She glanced at me, looked quickly away, and continued walking by. But after a few paces she paused and came to a stop. She turned her head slowly, frowned at me over her shoulder for a moment, then returned to stand before me. She took her time studying me, as if I were some new and curious sort of animal. But there was also something else in her eyes, something I could not quite understand, a trace of nervousness.

I said, "Don't tell me you didn't recognize me."

"Almost. I knew who it was but couldn't believe it. You've changed."

Of course, the bandages on my nose and forehead were gone, but I knew she meant it was more than that. There was the thin, white scar on my forehead and the break in my nose had not healed properly; it was twisted slightly to one side. But I had put on weight, too, and was deeply tanned and the wind and the sea and the sun had washed away the circles from under my eyes and the lines about my mouth. I was also wearing another suit and probably presented a more attractive picture than she remembered.

She tilted her head to one side and said, "Not bad. But it's funny, too. Now that you really are fishing it has made you look like anything but a fisherman. You look more what you really are, a well-groomed leech, but a healthy one."

"Word seems to be getting around. You've been talking to Gail?"

"I saw her one night."

"Stooge to the wealthy was her description."

"Same thing. So that was the kind of life you led?"

"So she and Matt seem to think. How about you?"

"They're probably right. It fits you better than anything else I can think of. You have a certain polish, you can be downright rude in a kind of polite way, you're nervy, and you certainly don't give a damn what anyone thinks of you. You're, well—" She groped for the right phrase, then said, "You're just too self-sufficient for an ordinary drifter."

"Funny, but I thought the same thing of you."

"What?"

"Too damned self-sufficient. That's what got under my skin the night your friends tossed me so impolitely out of the Las Olas."

She frowned at me, but with interest. "Really? Is that why you started that little fracas?"

"Well, that and my normal perversity. I was entertaining myself in a petty way, but I suppose I was also interested in seeing how much you could take."

Her eyes flamed angrily for a moment. "Well, you certainly found out."

"Didn't I, though? I can still feel that wet bar rag on my face."

She smiled, then started to laugh softly. "You really are a strange character." She nodded at the bundles and asked, "Carrying home your laundry?"

"No. These are new curtains for the house. I took that cottage you told me about. I put in a few things that made the old curtains look pretty awful, so I got some new ones."

"You would. Are you going to hang them yourself?"

There seemed to be a proposal in her question, so I said, "Well, I don't think I can do a very good job of it. That sort of thing usually needs the feminine touch."

She glanced at her wristwatch, then smiled and said, "All right. I have a little time."

I drove her to the cottage in the little coupé, parked under the pines, and led the way into the house. She had lived in the place for a few months the year before and knew it well. She noticed the changes and additions at once, but made no immediate comment other than a sharp glance at me. But when she opened the bundles and saw the glass-cloth draperies, she turned about to stare at me for a long moment. I had a hunch, later proved correct, that the draperies were probably much too expensive for the little place, or even for the whole neighborhood.

She removed a light cloth coat and tossed it over one of the chairs. She was wearing the usual off-the-shoulder, thin white blouse, a rather snug skirt, sheer nylons with a dark seam, and high-heeled shoes with a pencil-thin strap that accented the slimness of her ankles. She also wore a tantalizing perfume that tickled my nostrils and went considerably deeper.

We removed the rods from over all the windows and slid on the draperies. I helped her with that small task, but she did the actual hanging alone. She got up on a kitchen chair, stretched upward on her toes, and put the draperies properly in place. I stood aside and watched her, the long clean lines of her thighs, the pearlike curve of her hips, and the tight blouse over her breasts whenever she had to reach high. The snug skirt, too, was a bit awkward—she had to pull it above her knees every time she stepped up or down from the chair.

She was too busy to be aware of my concentration, or thoughts, but as she put up the last drape and stepped down to the floor, she turned and caught my gaze. She looked quickly away, but again I saw in her eyes the same small trace of nervousness that had been apparent on the street.

She stood in the middle of the living room, with a finger to her lips, studying the effect of the draperies, examined those in the bedroom for a moment, then returned to the living room. A tiny smile was playing about her lips. "The whole thing," she said, "is absolutely crazy. I like the way everything looks, but, really, this is no longer just a shack, or a fisherman's home. If any of the *Rosita* crew see this place they'll think you're a fairy."

"But you don't."

She glanced at me and again her eyes slid away. "No."

Her nervousness seemed to be increasing, so I went into the kitchen for ice and brought it out to the portable bar. She had seated herself on the couch and crossed her legs. She lit a cigarette, blew out a puff of smoke, and said that she would have a Martini. I mixed one for her, with a dividend in the bar glass, and a Scotch and soda for myself. I dropped to the couch at her side as she glanced at her watch.

"It's getting late. I have to be to work in another half hour."

"That's too bad. I was hoping this would be your night off."

Without turning her head, she looked sideways into my eyes. "Why?"

"Just an idea. I was thinking we might have dinner together here. It would be nice. Much better than going out somewhere." She sipped at her Martini without saying anything, her eyes still fixed on mine. I said, "Isn't it possible to get a substitute for the evening?"

She nodded. When I asked, "How much would you lose?" she replied, "About twenty dollars."

"That was my original investment in you."

She finished the Martini and got to her feet. She walked to the bar, filled her glass from the bar glass, and drank that down with her back to me. She slid her arms into the cloth coat, walked to the door, then paused and turned to look back at me. "May I borrow your car?"

I took the keys from my pocket and tossed them to her. She went out the door and closed it without another word. In a moment I heard the car start and drive away. I got up and fixed another highball.

An hour and a half later, a few minutes after six, I was slightly boiled and ready to leave the house for a tour of the bars. It looked as if my sudden plan for the evening had fizzled. But then I heard the car return and in another moment the click of high heels on the porch. I opened the door and Ginny came in, her arms loaded with packages. I took some of them from her and led the way into the kitchen.

"Sorry I took so long," she said, while unloading the packages on the drainboard. "I had trouble getting a girl to sub for me, then I had to go over to the Mediterranean Store in Carmel for the right kind of Provolone cheese." She asked brightly, "Do you like it? It's wonderful with cocktails. Nice bite."

I hadn't the faintest idea what Provolone cheese was but I said, "Sure."

"Then you mix some drinks while I get things ready."

She removed her coat with a nervous smile while I stirred another batch of Martinis. There was no need for her to explain that she had also gone home to change clothes. She was wearing red sandals, a longer pleated skirt, and a short-sleeved blouse with a decidedly lowcut V neckline. The bra she wore was strapless and the sheerest kind of ineffective covering. I wondered what it was all about. Our last meeting had been pretty tumultuous; I had made not the slightest kind of play for her on this occasion and she was on record as firmly wanting nothing whatever to do with a fisherman, yet she had deliberately clothed herself for our evening in the most provocative manner possible. I was lost in a fog of unanswered questions and contradictions.

She was right about the cheese. It had a very nice bite, indeed. She served it on crackers in the living room, with anchovies, pickles, Italian peppers, little onions, celery, and radishes. I settled back on the couch, munching at the appetizers and sipping at the Martini while watching her in the kitchen. I had my doubts about her culinary ability, but she seemed to know what she was doing and in short order came up with an Italian dinner of soup, salad, spaghetti and meat balls, toasted garlic bread, and a bottle of pinot noir. We ate at a card table in the living room. The dinner was excellent.

She was pleased that I had enjoyed it and explained, "My mother was a good cook. Mrs. Martinelli has taught me all kinds of things, too." She sat back, lit a cigarette, and watched me through the smoke. "You like good food, don't you?"

"I suppose anyone does."

"But you more than most people. Matt has told me

that you don't really know very much about cooking, but he and the rest of the crew are eating better than they ever have."

"I guess I enjoy experimenting."

"No, that isn't it. What you're trying to do on that boat is prepare the kind of food you're used to."

I finished my glass of wine and left the table to turn on the radio to a platter program. "That isn't a bad observation, Ginny."

She waved her hand about to indicate the new furniture and prints and draperies. "You like everything better. You're used to everything being better. Those draperies, for example. No one else would spend that kind of money to hang glass-cloth in a shack like this. But you do because you have to. You have to have things the way you're used to seeing them." She paused, sipped at her wine, then asked softly, "What are you running from, Tom?"

I moved away to the bar, poured brandy into a snifter glass, which also made her smile, then dropped back on the couch. I glanced at her, still seated at the table, and said, "I'm not running. My private little engine has come about dead-center."

"I don't think so. You're either running or hiding from something." She left the table, helped herself to the brandy and settled on the couch at my side. "Remember what I said about you being a leech and Gail and Matt thinking you were a stooge to the wealthy?"

"Yes."

"It isn't true. You aren't the type at all. I've felt something different about you ever since we talked that first night on the bridge of the *Rosita*. You're scared, yes. I sensed it then. Something has you badly worried."

"Just myself."

"I don't know." She gave me a sympathetic smile and asked, "You don't mind my going on this way?"

"No. No, not at all."

"All right." She took a deep breath and said, "I think you're hiding out from the police."

My heart skipped a beat and the palms of my hands were damp. But I managed a phony smile and said, "Now, Ginny, really—"

She said stubbornly, "I'm convinced that's it. But you don't have to tell me—if you don't want to."

"I'm not going to."

"I didn't think you would. But if I were you I'd manage a few lies to stop everyone from guessing about you."

"You really do believe I'm in trouble."

"Yes. You've had a decent background somewhere, better than most of us. You're used to really good living. No one throws over anything like that to wind up on a stinking fishing boat just for a lark."

"I haven't, either." For some unaccountable and impulsive reason I started to tell her, "There was a young woman who died—"

But that was as far as I got. Ginny's hand flew out and closed on my mouth. "No!" she cried. "I knew it was something like that. But don't tell me. I don't want to know."

I stared at her, amazed. There was nothing imaginary about the depth and intensity of her concern. The gesture of stopping my words had been too spontaneous and the light of sympathy in her dark eyes was too real. But there was also something else in her eyes. A yearning of some kind? But, God, that couldn't be. At least, not for me.

When her hand slid from my lips, I said, "I appreciate your attitude, Ginny."

"Don't say anything about it."

"Then you have me puzzled. Obviously, you've given some thought to my character. I don't get it. I don't even understand why you accepted this little date for the evening. On the Carmel beach you told me that as far as you were concerned I had the plague."

She leaned her head against the back of the couch, her black hair tumbling loosely over smooth, white shoulders. She closed her eyes and said huskily, "I know. I even meant it, at the time. And I knew it was no good because I think I started liking you when we first talked together. I knew, then, you were different than anyone I'd ever known."

I leaned toward her and asked, "Is that all it is, just liking?"

She made no reply.

I looked down at her and slowly lowered my lips until they touched hers. Her arms slid about my shoulders and she pressed her lips hungrily against mine and arched her body so that my arms could go about her waist. I felt hot blood pounding in my temples and pulled away from her lips to whisper, "And you don't care that I'm hiding from the police?"

She shook her head. "No."

"You don't even care about my being a fisherman?"

"No," she cried, her fingers biting into my shoulders. "My God, I don't seem to care about anything."

I got up, flicked off the lights, then lifted her in my arms and carried her into the bedroom.

I had thought that, even though sex seemed to emanate from every cell of her lush body, she was perhaps a cold or even frigid woman. Some women are like that. But I could not have been more wrong. Ginny giving herself was like the eruption of a volcano. There was nothing withdrawn or withheld. She gave herself completely, without reservation, with vigor and passion that matched and even surpassed her appearance. There was wildness in her passion and tears and the bite of her fingernails and also a vast well of tenderness and the extremely feminine desire to be conquered.

Once, in the middle of the night, she sighed and said, "I knew it would be like this. I intended it to be like this. I have always intended it to be like this. And now it is."

At the first hint of dawn, just before we fell asleep, she turned into my arms and whispered, "I guess you think I'm crazy. Maybe I am. Or maybe you even think I'm a tramp. I'm not that, but you don't have to say anything about it one way or the other. You don't have to love me. You don't even have to pretend and say that you do just to make me feel better. I feel all right. You don't have to make me feel any way but the way I feel right now, and I can feel this way without you lying about it."

"Are you in love, Ginny?"

She laughed softly and said, "I've been in love ever

since I hit you in the face with a wet bar rag."

I closed my eyes, happy and content in a way, but wondering what sort of crazy world I had got myself into.

CHAPTER EIGHT

I was awakened a little after nine in the morning by a fist banging on the front door. I got out of bed and staggered sleepily through the living room, my mind not working at all, to open the front door. Tony was standing there in his work clothes, frowning irritably at me as I stood there.

He exploded angrily, "Geez, Howie, why don't you put a phone in this dump? I gotta leave work and come all the way up here to get you."

"What's the matter?"

"Matter! You got rocks in your head? We been on the boat since seven, waiting for you, so we can go out to the nets. Geez, let's get moving."

"Oh. Sorry. I—ah—forgot. Overslept a little."

"Yeah."

His eyes then swung beyond me and for the first time saw the disorder of the living room, the empty glasses, and the table set for two with the remains of the dinner still on it. But he also saw Ginny's coat and purse and a sly grin broke through his swarthy features.

"Well, well. Had some company, huh?"

Unfortunately, before I could get in the way, he looked toward the open bedroom door and saw Ginny's coal-black hair on the pillow. Her back was toward us, but there was no mistaking her identity. Tony's eyes opened wide, then closed narrowly with what appeared to be frustration and resentment. He looked sharply at me, his lips thin and his eyes burning.

I stepped before him and said, "I'll see you at the boat," then slammed the door in his face. He remained where he was for a while, and it was a minute or so before I heard him turn and leave the porch. I swore under my breath and went back to the bedroom.

Ginny rolled over and opened her eyes to watch me as I dressed in a flannel shirt and sweater, a long-billed cap, Levis, and knee-high rubber boots. She yawned and smiled and reached up her arms to pull me down when I leaned over the bed.

I told her, "You go back to sleep and leave when you want. There's another key hanging on the window frame in the kitchen. Do you want it?"

"Yes."

"Okay. Take it with you."

She caressed the back of my neck with her fingers and smiled into my eyes. "Who were you just talking to?"

"Tony."

"Oh?"

"I guess Matt sent him after me."

"Did he—?"

"I'm afraid so. The bedroom door was open. I just wasn't thinking."

She shrugged a lovely white shoulder and sighed, "Who cares? They'd be talking about us pretty soon, anyway. Tom?"

"Yes?"

"Should I move in with you? Do you want me to?"

"Good God, no! Look, darling, if you did a thing like that you really would be an outcast."

She said impatiently, "I don't care. Everybody talks about me, anyway. Now it can be the truth for a change. But if you don't want me to—"

"I don't."

"Oh. Well, how long are you going to be gone?"

"Two or three days."

She pulled me down until my face was between her breasts and whispered, "That's a long time."

I pushed away and straightened up with a laugh that was probably pretty shaky. "I'm no superman, darling. I'll see you the moment I get back."

It was not easy turning away from her and walking out of that house. One of my more difficult accomplishments to date.

The moment I stepped onto the deck of the Rosita I knew that Tony had been talking. Pete gave me a sly look and even the impassive Johnson grinned as I went by him into the cabin. Matt got up from one of the benches, stared at me for a long moment in cold silence that bordered on hostility, then walked out of the galley to go up to the open bridge. We got underway at once, cut around the harbor's breakwater and headed out through the bay to the open sea. Tony came inside to help me peel potatoes, a job which he usually shunned.

"Quite a place you got there," he said. "That place of yours looks all right."

"I like it."

"Yeah. Kind of dolled it up a bit, didn't you? And you didn't take long getting yourself on the list, neither."

"What list?"

"Ginny's."

"Why, you no-good bastard—"

He laughed and sneered, "My, we're touchy, ain't we? Listen, chum, you ain't been around here long. I know the score and you don't. That queen's been shacking around ever since I've known her and that's when she was a kid."

"You're a goddamned liar."

"Oh, yeah? Ask anybody. Ask Matt."

"He has already told me what he thinks. Because an ignorant bunch of jerks like you couldn't make the grade you've run off at the mouth to give her a shady reputation."

"I ain't given her nothing. All you gotta do is take a look at her. You ever see any other doll look sexier?"

There was no answer to that. Tony figured he had scored some sort of victory and burst into a laugh. He slapped me on the back and said, "No hard feelings, huh?" Then he looked almost sad as he whispered, more to himself than to me, "Man, I'll bet that's really something in bed."

I had to get away from him, or a few more words would have started a bloody brawl. I went out to the deck and forward to watch the bow cutting through the water. I turned to glance up at the open bridge and saw Matt, at the wheel, looking down at me. He jerked his head for me to come up. I went up the iron rungs and stood at his side, leaning back against the spray shelter. Wearing sea boots, a leather windbreaker, and a scarf around his neck, he looked more of a giant than ever.

Without looking at me, his eyes fixed on the far horizon, he asked, "Tony give you a bad time?"

"He tried."

"He would. And he'll keep trying. I'm not asking you if what he had to say is true. There is no doubt that it is. He wouldn't make up a thing like that. Not about you. Himself, yes, but not you. He made a pass at Ginny once and got his face scratched. He's been burning ever since. Now he'll take it out on you. So I guess we get rid of him. He's a damned good fisherman, I'd hate to lose him, but I suppose he'll have to go."

I thought about it and shook my head. "I'd rather he stayed. I can handle Tony."

Matt turned to look at me, his expression no longer quite so hostile. He looked me up and down and nodded. "Maybe you can, now. Okay. He stays. But you'd better have it out with him damned soon, or everything will get out of hand."

"I will."

Matt looked away from me and was silent for a long while. But when we were rounding the point he said, "She must have fallen in love with you."

"So she claims."

"It would have to be that. I've known Ginny too long. I've been trying to figure it out. That's the only answer that makes sense. She fell in love." He lifted a big hand, slammed it down on the wheel and roared into space, "Geez, what a dirty, rotten break for the kid!"

I suppose I stared at him with my mouth wide open,

because after a while I got it closed and managed to swallow. "Just what the devil do you mean by that?"

"Just what I said, damn it. You're about the most fouled-up character I've ever run across. It's all right for me to like you, I guess I do, in a way, but not for a person like Ginny. She's had it rough enough. All her life she's had it rough. Now you have to come along."

"Hey, wait a minute. You're not talking about a child, you know."

"She's nineteen."

"So what? She's more of a woman than any woman I've ever known."

"You know what I mean. She doesn't know how to cope with characters like you."

I was getting exasperated and said, "It makes me so happy to see everyone taking such a charming interest in my affairs. Maybe you and I had better have it out, too. My personal life is none of your damned business. Understand?"

I fully expected him to make an issue of it and perhaps slap me around, but, peculiarly, he shrugged and turned his attention back to the course. There was only one answer to that, an answer I did not like to accept, as it lessened his stature in my eyes, but I had to take it. We were more or less partners in the shark enterprise. Matters were going well and Matt was getting on his feet. His ambitions were moving along. But the boat charter was in my name and forcing an issue with me could cause a rupture and a delay in Matt's plans. His ambition took precedence over everything else. He was even willing to back down.

I turned away, momentarily disgusted, and went below deck.

Tony and I had it out three days later, as we were returning to port. We had a good haul in the nets and the decks were loaded with shark. Johnson was at the wheel, while the rest of us were gutting out the shark livers and slicing off the ventral fins. As usual, the deck was red with blood and deep in fish and guts. I was still not used to that phase of the business and, though I could handle it as well as the others, I had to force myself. My stomach, however, was doing flip-flops and I was swearing under my breath with every slice of the knife.

We finished the job just as we were rounding Point Pinos into the bay. Pete leaned back against a hatch cover to light a cigarette with bloody fingers as Matt uncoiled the hose to wash off the deck. Tony straightened up, stretched his arms, looked toward Pacific Grove and Monterey, then grinned at me.

"Hey there, Howie, we're almost home."

I looked over my shoulder at Pacific Grove, which we were passing, and nodded. "It's always good to get back."

"Yeah," he said. "Specially for you. If I had a woman like yours, I'd start swimming for land right about here."

"Listen, Tony—"

He ignored me and went on, "No kidding, brother, that's really something. Why, I knew a guy once was with her—"

I dropped the knife I was holding, skidded toward him through the blood, and smashed him across the mouth. He slipped and sprawled out over the fish, but was instantly back on his feet, no longer smiling, his eyes cold and vicious. He swung at me with his left and I ducked under to land my left in the pit of his stomach and a hard right that grazed his temple. He caught me in the face with a blow that rocked me down to my heels and started to swing his right.

Matt roared, "Tony! For God's sake, Tony, the knife."

Tony's reflexes were fortunately perfect. A slight shift of his body and his right fist fanned the air an inch from my face. He stepped back and looked at the fish knife in his right hand, which he had forgotten he was holding. His face paled, but for a moment only. He threw the knife aside, screamed something foul and came at me in a rush.

It was not like it had been before. I had toughened and hardened in every way and balanced Tony in weight and height. But I also had the advantage of having been taught boxing, even as a small boy, by the most expensive instructors in the business. That advantage was not particularly noticeable on that bloody deck, but it was a help. I could not bob and weave about, but I was better able to defend myself, even so, and suffered less damage than Tony. He got through a few times to knock me sprawling into the mess on deck and twice booted me when I was down. I felt as if all my ribs were broken, but they remained intact.

Tony had a bad habit of telegraphing a right punch by jerking his head down each time he let it go. I spotted the failing and made full use of it. Every time his head went down I stepped inside, caught him off balance, and smashed him in the face at least three or four times before he could cover up again. He had no idea what was wrong and simply kept boring in, repeating the same mistake over and over again. But he kept coming, the two of us covered with blood and some of it our own. Eventually, though, he had to weaken. His arms began to drop and he was soon incapable of protecting himself in any manner. I set myself and hit him flush on the chin with a right that numbed my arm to the shoulder. Tony fell face forward on the deck and lay still.

I leaned back against the cabin, hungrily sucking volumes of air into my aching and burning lungs. Matt turned on the sea hose and smashed me against the wall with the force of the water. But it felt good and I turned slowly about to get all the blood off my clothes. Tony received the same treatment. The moment he sat up Matt turned the hose on him. When he got to his feet, Matt calmly turned away to wash off the deck.

Tony stood there weaving a bit and staring at me and fooling three cavities in his mouth where teeth had been. He looked over his shoulder at Matt and asked, "I guess I go?"

Matt shrugged and jerked his head toward me. "It's up to Tom."

"Then I go."

I said, "Not if you don't want to."

"No?"

"No. Now you know where you stand, I'd rather you stayed with us."

He stared at me, puzzled for a moment, then nodded.

"Okay. It's a good boat. I'll stay."

All of us got back to work cleaning the deck and stacking the fish in place for unloading. I could feel every bruise on my body where Tony had connected and every move I made was painful. I thought of Ginny in bed, the way I had left her, and wearily shook my head. I wondered if I was getting anywhere—or just being a damned fool.

CHAPTER NINE

As soon as we had the boat secured and the fish and cans unloaded, I took off for my cottage and soaked for long, blissful minutes under a warm shower. I looked around the place, while dressing in sports clothes, and saw that Ginny had left it in immaculate condition. She had also left a perfumed handkerchief on the bed cover, an obvious little reminder. I touched it to my nose, thinking of her and how she had been, then put it away in a drawer.

I drove downtown to a drugstore and looked up the Martinelli number in the telephone book. A woman, apparently Mrs. Martinelli, answered the phone and explained in broken English that Ginny was away, she did not know where, for the afternoon. I felt like tearing the phone from the wall when I hung up. I had been so confident that in another few minutes I would have her again in my arms.

I walked out into the sunshine, wondering what to do, and decided to buy another suit. I went into a men's shop, where there was an excellent tailor, looked through a whole rack of suits and finally selected a single-breasted undyed Shetland with patch pockets. The trousers had to be tried on and fitted, so the salesman told me to go to the rear and take the dressing booth on the right. I walked to the back of the shop, but unthinkingly turned left instead of right.

When I pushed the curtain aside Gail was standing in the booth, just about to step into a pair of slacks. Her skirt was hanging behind her on a hook. I had a quick glimpse of long legs in sheer nylons, a garter belt, and powder-blue lace panties before she turned her head and saw me. She stared at me, her eyes open wide, too astonished to cover up. I grinned and apologized and backed out.

Later I waited for her on the sidewalk in front of the shop and walked down the street with her. She explained nervously that she always had her slacks made in that shop, that only a men's tailor knew how to do the job properly. Then she suddenly lost her embarrassment and began to laugh.

"I guess," she said, "I must have looked like the well-known startled fawn."

"And a very lovely one."

"Oh?" She gave me that quick, sidewise glance of hers, the constant search for approval. But it no longer irritated me.

We went into a hardware shop, where she purchased some light bulbs, an extension cord and a number of other items for her house. While waiting for them to be wrapped, she said, "I saw Matt a little while ago. He tells me you two are making a killing with sharks."

"I suppose we are."

"He also says you're a remarkably handy man to have on a fishing boat."

"That's high praise from Matt."

"Yes, it is. Going with you has certainly changed his streak of bad luck. Is that a trait of yours, bringing good luck to other people?"

I thought of how it had been the reverse of that all my life and shook my head. "That's a recent development."

"Well, there is no doubt you have changed his luck. But, you know, I still can't picture you on a fishing boat."

"Does it require a certain type?"

"Whatever it requires, you aren't it."

"But Matt is?"

She frowned and said thoughtfully, almost regretfully, "He's a born fisherman and always will be one."

"You don't like that."

"Well—"

"Matt is the kind of man you'd rather have, isn't he? But he's in the wrong end of the business. So you'll settle for an obnoxious character such as Steve Moore."

She frowned at me and snapped, "Are you going out of your way to be nasty again?"

"I wasn't aware of it. I'm just curious about you."

"Why?"

"Well, you interest me. But my interest, you understand, is purely academic."

She took the package from the clerk, then turned to smile lightly at me. "Are you sure?"

"Quite sure. You're very lovely, you're even a beautiful

woman, and I have no doubt that your character is exemplary, but there is something badly out of focus. I think you've acquired a peculiarly distorted sense of values."

She spun away from me and started out of the store, her high heels clicking angrily on the floor. I followed her out to the sidewalk, thinking that she would simply walk on and away, but she came to a halt and turned to face me. Surprisingly, there was no anger whatever in her expression.

She placed a hand on my arm and asked, "Would you still like that dinner date?"

I was so startled that I stammered, "Well, I—yes, of course."

"All right. Suppose you pick me up at my house at— let's see—shall we say six-ish?"

That "six-ish" almost made me burst into a laugh, but I stifled that and said, "Fine, I'll be there."

It wasn't until she had walked away and I had started down the street for a bar that I remembered it was Ginny I was anxious to see that evening, not Gail. But, then, I could make an early evening of it, drop Gail at her home, and pick up Ginny at the Las Olas at closing time.

I phoned the cocktail room shortly after five, got Ginny on the wire and told her I would see her when she was through. She suggested getting a substitute and spending the evening with me, but I said quickly that I had some other things to do and hung up before she could protest.

It was fortunate that I'd changed to a flannel suit, as when I picked up Gail at her home she was really dressed for the evening in a full-skirted short organdy, with rounded sleeves that dropped off her shoulders, and a neckline cut as low as anything Ginny would dare wear. She looked like and had all the polish and poise of a professional manikin as she left her house and walked to my car. I did a little rapid thinking, trying to change my plans from a casual dinner date to something a bit more elaborate. Gail made up my mind with a request that we go to Del Monte Lodge.

During the short drive over the hill and through Del Monte Forest to Pebble Beach I worried over the possibility of being recognized. I had stopped at the Lodge dozens of times, had given many parties there, knew Sam Morse, the baron of Pebble Beach, rather well and was certainly known by most of the staff. Well, I thought, here is where I may have to do some real bluffing to keep my little masquerade going.

I did come close to one danger, but no one actually recognized me. When we walked into the cocktail room two of the bartenders started to give me smiles of recognition, but, after a second glance, apparently decided that they did not know me, after all. We took a small table against the back wall, facing toward the large windows, and ordered Gibsons in the rough. I was just lifting the first drink when a familiar figure came in from the outer door and started through the room toward the hallway. It was George Finley, of the Finley Steel and Cable Company, a neighbor of mine in Bel Air. There was no time for me to turn away. He saw me when he got halfway across the room, came to a pause and stared at me. But the scar on my forehead, the slightly broken twist of my nose and the deep burning of sun and sea must have changed my appearance even more than I had realized. He stood there frowning and blinking at me, then suddenly smiled shyly as if embarrassed at being caught staring at a stranger and walked on and out of the room. I let out my breath and uncrossed my fingers.

Gail asked, "Did you know that man?"

"No."

"He seemed to think he knew you, for a minute, anyway."

"I probably look like someone else he knows."

"I guess."

We had a number of Gibsons, a fine way to ruin dinner, then went into the dining room, which was about half filled. Again, one of the waitresses thought she recognized me and scurried about to get us a choice table at the windows overlooking the eighteenth green of the Pebble Beach golf course and the ocean. It was not until we were seated that the waitress frowned, then gave me an apologetic little smile.

"You know," she said, "I thought you were a man who comes up here from Los Angeles once in a while, a Mr. Carleton. Then I just remembered he died in some sort of accident. So," she giggled, "you couldn't be him, could you?"

Gail was staring at me with a narrowed, thoughtful expression, but at that moment her attention was diverted elsewhere. Steve Moore came into the dining room with four middle-aged couples and took a reserved table not far from ours. Moore and the other men were wearing dinner jackets and the women were dowdily gowned in overdone evening dress. They appeared as if they were grimly going to enjoy themselves if they had to fight for it.

Gail gasped, leaned toward me and whispered, "I forgot this is where they were going. Steve wanted me to be in the party, but I begged off with a fake headache. Now he's going to be angry."

I nodded my head toward the group and asked, "What's the occasion?"

"They're all in the produce game. Steve has some sort of deal on with them. If we have another bad pilchard season I think he intends switching his cannery to packing produce."

Moore was beaming at his guests as they were all seated, but when he turned and saw Gail his expansive grin faded to a wry grimace. Then, when he saw me, his face flamed red and his little pig eyes blazed with frustration and anger. He jerked his glance away almost as if he had been slapped. But in another moment his loud voice was booming throughout the room and he was knocking himself out playing the gracious host.

I glanced at Gail and had to smile. She was looking smug and complacent. She could not have selected a better partner for the evening than I to dangle in Moore's face. It was amusing, even though I was deliberately being used.

She chatted away gaily through dinner, compelling me to pay close attention to her, and laughed rather too often at remarks I made that were never that humorous. Moore watched the show she was putting on and could not help but come to the conclusion that she was having a simply wonderful time. Actually, it was very entertaining.

When we had finished dinner I thought we would still remain in the dining room for a number of brandies, then leave shortly after Moore's party. Gail's sense of timing, however, was better than that. She got up to leave the moment we had finished coffee. She had needled Moore just enough to make him jealous. Enough was enough. She smiled and waved her fingers at him as we left the room. The poor slob was literally sweating.

We went into Carmel and had brandies at the Pine Inn bar, went up the street to Whitney's to switch over to highballs, then drove out to the Mission Ranch Club on the edge of town, where we could dance. I was more than a little conscious of Gail's supple body in my arms, her firm breasts against my chest and the animal flexibility of her waist under my palm. She was an excellent dancer, so good, in fact, that I forgot all about time.

It was close to one a.m. when I glanced at my watch and remembered Ginny. We had another round of drinks, one more dance and left. Gail was tired and almost, but not quite, leaned against me in the car on the drive back. At her home, I got out of the car and waited with her as she unlocked the front door.

When the door opened, she turned to smile at me and placed a hand on my arm. "Good night, Tom. It's been very nice."

I placed my hands on her waist and looked down into her eyes and then my arms were about her. She clung to me a moment as I kissed her, her hands on my shoulders, then pushed me away.

She laughed and said exactly what I knew she would say, "Why, Tom, you've lost your academic approach."

"Of course. Isn't that what you've been after all evening?"

Her smile twisted and for a moment her face was pale. I pulled her to me and kissed her again, holding her tightly. She made no attempt to push me away. When I dropped my arms she stepped back and looked into my eyes for a moment, then turned and went inside, closing the door softly behind her.

I drove away and got to the Las Olas as quickly as I could. Ginny was not there. The bartender informed me that she had waited until twelve-thirty, then had gone. I drove to my place, feeling something close to panic, pulled into the parking place under the pines and looked toward the cottage. The lights were on in the living room. I heaved a sigh of relief, wiped the lipstick from my mouth and got out of the car.

Ginny was waiting for me, lying on the couch, smoking, a highball in her other hand. She was not yet tight, but her heavy lids gave away the information that she was not far from it. The radio was blaring loudly and a newly opened bottle of bourbon on the bar had quite a dent in it. I turned down the radio and took the glass from Ginny's hand to empty it in the sink. Her eyes followed me into the kitchen and back. When I stood before the couch she moved her hips over to make room for me. I sat down and put an arm about her waist.

She asked huskily, "Have a good time?"

"We caught a lot of fish."

"I mean tonight."

Something warned me not to lie, so I shrugged and said, "Fair. It was all right."

"Seems to me it would be better than that."

"Why?"

"Well, for one thing, she's beautiful. At least," she qualified, "everyone seems to think so. And for another, she's got quite a body and she knows how to throw it around."

"Now, wait a minute—"

She sucked in her breath sharply and asked bluntly, "Is she better in bed than I am? Is that it?"

I looked into her eyes and saw that she was deliberately torturing herself. "Now, look," I said, "you're getting yourself all upset over nothing."

She blinked her lids to hold back tears and asked, "I am? I don't think so. You've been gone three days. I've been going crazy for you to get back. So you call and tell me you're busy for the evening and you'll see me later and I'm dying to see you right then. So some people come in the bar just before quitting time and tell me they saw you with Gail at the Lodge and the Mission Ranch. What am I to think then?" A tear spilled over and ran down her cheek. She brushed it away and said, "I guess the first person you're dying to see when you get back is Gail."

I could not help but smile and leaned over to kiss the tip of her nose. "It wasn't that way, darling. I tried to get you as soon as I got home, but you were out. Mrs. Martinelli didn't know where you were."

Ginny's eyes started to come alive. "I didn't know that."

"She'll tell you I called. Then I ran into Gail downtown. We thought it would be a good idea to have dinner together. Frankly, though it may not be gentlemanly to say so, I was euchred into it. I thought I could get away early. Gail, however, had other plans."

Ginny lifted her head and snapped out viciously, "She would, that bitch. She—"

"Now, hold on. Not those kind of plans." I told her about the Lodge and Steve Moore, but failed to explain that the Moore party did not also continue on to Mission Ranch. "So you see how it was? I was being used as bait to make Steve Moore jealous. That's the way it happened and I'm damned sorry I was late."

She thought it over, accepted it, then said, "You know, Steve is really going to hate the ground you walk on. Not just because you were out with Gail. He's been drooling around me for years and one of these days he's going to learn about us. My God," she said and laughed. "Will he blow his top!"

She looked up into my eyes and her own eyes went soft as I lowered my head and our lips crushed together. Under my chest I could feel her fingers fumbling with the snaps of her blouse. There was no longer anything to talk about.

CHAPTER TEN

The following day, when I boarded the *Rosita*, Matt had me follow him up to the bridge of the boat where we would be away from the crew. It was a gloomy, overcast day with a low bank of fog lying just off the breakwater. All of the fishing boats were at their moorings, crowding the small harbor. I sat on the helmsman's bench and looked up at Matt's giant outline against the fog. His lips were a thin line, his eyes were narrowed to cold, blue slits and tiny muscles worked along his lean jaws. I wondered what had caused him to come to a boil and learned that I was the reason. He had heard about me taking Gail out the night before.

"I know what you think of her," he said, a dangerous edge to his voice. "I know what you think of all of us. Your attitude's pretty obvious. We're all scum."

"You're wrong, Matt. Maybe, at first—"

"Look, chum; I'm doing the talking."

I shrugged and lit a cigarette and blew the smoke in his face. The muscles along his jaw quivered with rage, but he controlled himself and even managed a cold smile.

"That's typical of you. You know I can smash you to jelly, so you go out of your way to see how close you can get without being smashed."

"Maybe I don't care."

"You care, all right. It's just— Aw, the hell with it. I was talking about Gail. I don't want you making a play for her."

I leaned back with my arms over the spray shield and asked him, "Why should I be the sole exception in Monterey? Seems to me everyone is making a play for her, including you and Steve Moore. And from where I sit Moore has the inside track. So why do you worry about me, assuming you know what you're talking about?"

"Because of what happened to Ginny. That shouldn't happen to a dog, but it did. Gail has also never known anyone like you. Moore is a symbol. I'm a symbol. All the people she knows are symbols of something or other. Easy to put your finger on, to know where you stand and how they stand. But you represent nothing known to her. You're as complicated to her as you are to Ginny. I know. She's talked to me about you."

"That must have been interesting."

"It was. We've hauled you over between us more than once. You're no fisherman, yet you have a hell of a knowledge of fish and the sea. I doubt if you've ever actually worked on a boat before, but you know how to handle a boat as well as I do and you read charts like the Sunday funnies. You know more about navigation than anyone in the damned fleet. It's screwy. I picked you up in San Pedro, evidently a drunken bum cut up in a lousy brawl, and you turn out to be perfectly at home in the more expensive places as well as the dives. You don't seem to belong anywhere and you're at ease everywhere. That fascinates a woman like Gail."

I started to laugh. "She isn't fascinated by me, Matt. All she wants is for me to keel over and salaam to her beauty. She needs that from every man she meets. She has to have it. But once that is accomplished I no longer count."

"You sure have a peculiar way of figuring her out."

"I'm not in love with her."

He looked away from me into the fog and stated simply, "I am. Always have been."

"Is she aware of that?"

He shrugged and nodded. "Oh, sure. How could she miss? But so far it hasn't counted with her. I think it will soon, though. I have a hunch the sardines will be back this season."

"Such a low-caste word. Gail always refers to them as pilchards."

"Yeah. Anyway, if they do come back and I can break into the sardine fleet I can clean up. That will make the difference. And if I get on my feet there I can help straighten out her cannery."

"You know that end of the business?"

"God, yes. Inside and out. Gail's been after me all along to run the cannery for her, but I can't go for that until I get on my own feet first."

"How about Moore?"

He frowned and said uneasily, "I don't know how that's going. But I know one thing; only two things about him interest her, his money and his power. I don't think that Steve, as an individual, interests her at all."

"Holy Mary and all the rest of it. What a sweet character that makes of her."

"I still say I don't blame her. If I get on my own feet—I know she likes me—we get along—" He paused thoughtfully for a second, then turned to glower down at me. "Meanwhile, I don't want you in the way. Only one thing about Gail, or any other woman, could interest you."

"You're a trusting soul."

"I don't trust you any farther than I can throw this boat."

"My ever-loving partner."

"Say, look; you were the one pulled that rotten deal on Oka. It couldn't be anyone else. Now he's nothing but a bum."

"He was a bum before. What's the difference in degree?"

"Before he at least had something to hang onto. Now he's let go all the way. Now he's never out of a bar. Funny thing," he mused, "but our success with his nets is completing his ruin. Now he can afford to stay drunk all the time." He took a deep breath and sighed. "Anyway, you stay away from Gail. That I won't go for."

"And if I don't?"

He looked down at me as he would an insect. "Then I'll smash you."

I got to my feet and flipped the cigarette over the side. "You know, Matt, I like you. You're about as close to being a friend as I've ever had. So I'd really hate to ask you to get off the boat. I trust you haven't forgotten the charter is in my name."

He stood before me, his hands clenching and unclenching to control his temper. He hadn't forgotten.

"There is also something else," I said. "I've been giving a little thought on how to break into the sardine fleet. It can be done. I mean, we can do it together. But without me I don't think you have a prayer. In other words, Matt, you can't continue shark fishing and you can't get into sardines unless you string along with me. So think it over and let's not hear any more chatter about who is going to smash whom. I live my life as I damned well please and I take orders from no one."

I waited for him to say something, but as he stood there simply staring at me I turned away and went below. I went into the skipper's stateroom, forward in the main cabin, tuned the radio to some crooner or other and stretched out on the lower bunk. I may have appeared relaxed, which is what I was striving for, but inwardly I was jelly.

Matt came by and paused to look in the door.

"Thought it over?" I asked.

He nodded. "It didn't take much thinking."

"I figured that. So now we can concentrate on sardines?"

"That's right. You work it out. You should have some pretty beautiful angles."

"I have. But about the ravishing Gail Norton—?"

He stared in at me on the bunk, then turned on his heel and left without a word. The victory was hollow and cheap. Matt, I believed, meant more to me than a hundred Gail Nortons. It would have been so easy to put him straight and even have him laughing about it. Only the smell of danger, the compulsion to face the battering rams of his fists, had forced me to make an issue of it. It had not been Gail. It had been the same old story. It was always the same.

I felt drained and empty and enervated. God, I wondered, could I never lose that self-disgust? Was it impossible for me to do something that would make me feel proud, even a small accomplishment that I could call good? Must I always live with a wish to destroy a self that had been born on a mountain top, ashamed that there had been no personal effort in the achievement and that the mountain had simply been handed to me? It seemed so. Even as Tom Howie it was still the same.

Gail Norton was nothing. So, very well, I thought, amending the idea, I would like her to think well of Tom Howie, fisherman. Perhaps there was even physical desire mixed up in it somewhere. But other than that she was nothing. She was, in fact, even highly amusing. It was entertaining to think of her striving and yearning and seeking for everything I actually represented. It made me chuckle to picture her reaction if she learned that I was really Carleton, representative of a wealth she could not even dream about. That was a sadly comic picture, Gail searching wildly, almost frantically, for something that could easily be given to her by a man she was constantly rubbing elbows with, yet never aware of it. It was incongruous and it was funny, too, in a rather sad way.

But, even so, I had to admit, she was interesting in others ways, too. At least, she knew what she wanted out of life, which was more than I could say for myself. She had purpose and she had direction. Perhaps Matt was not too wrong about her, after all.

I cupped my hands behind my neck, stared at the timbers overhead, and thought of Gail Norton.

CHAPTER ELEVEN

The sardine season was getting too close for Matt's comfort, so he decided to make one last, big haul of shark. While we were on a trip off Big Sur he explained how it could be done—with luck. All the nets could be fastened together, taken a hundred or more miles to sea, then used as a drift net. It was the dangerous way to fish—there was weather to contend with and the nets would be drifting in the steamer lanes—but sometimes the results with a drift net were spectacular. It was worth taking the gamble.

But when he said we would be gone for weeks, or even over a month, I suggested that I stay ashore and work on the sardine deal. What I had in mind was also tricky, but I refused to explain it to Matt. He cynically assumed that there was something dirty about it and did not press me.

"It's okay," he said. "You figure the angles. We'll have to put on a man to take your place, but you'll get your share from the livers, too."

"How, if I'm not along?"

"You just leave your fishing clothes aboard and you automatically share in the haul. That's fishing law."

"Very convenient. Then it's settled?"

"Sure."

When we took in the nets out of the sea we left them aboard and returned to Monterey. The nets were overhauled and fastened together and stored on the stern. We put in a load of provisions and got the boat in shape for a long trip and Matt was ready to go. I stood on the wharf at dawn one morning and watched the *Rosita* leave for sea. It was almost as if a part of me was sailing away. Matt looked back at me from the bridge, worried lines about his eyes and mouth. He was obviously thinking of Gail. I was worried too, but about another matter. What I had in mind could easily backfire and explode me back into a life where I would be a hunted fugitive.

In my wallet was a small royalty check for thirty-one thousand dollars made out to T. Howard Carleton from the funds of the Carleton Petroleum Company. I had picked up the check a few days before the accident in the Jaguar, but had never banked it. That check was still legally good.

As soon as Matt had gone, I returned to my cottage; got the check out of the wallet, then went to the Monterey Bank when the doors opened. I had an account there of slightly better than eight thousand dollars from the proceeds of shark livers. I endorsed the back of the check with my correct signature, then underneath signed Thomas Howie with a heavy backhand slant, an affectation of writing I was using in Monterey. I made out a deposit slip and gave the check and the slip to the teller. Her eyebrows lifted with surprise at the amount of the check, but she wrote the figure in my pass book and initialed it without comment. But that, I knew, would not be the end of it. It was not reasonable to expect a check of that size to turn up at that late date. I would definitely hear about it.

It was a tremendous risk for me to take and even a gamble that could have fatal consequences. But I had a plan worked out that I was rather sure would succeed. The risk was worth taking. Success would mean a better standing in the brotherhood of the sea, would secure the name of Tom Howie and would allow my masquerade to continue in safety. There was no longer any question in my mind of ever attempting a return to my former position in society. Accidentally, or otherwise, I had killed another person. Any jury would take a dim view of me and the particular circumstances of that night. So possibly a skilled battery of attorneys could get me off with a life sentence. And what would that be like, living in a concrete tomb, waiting simply to die? No, I realized, I could never take a risk such as that, regardless of the Carleton millions involved. It was far better to make one gamble toward the start of another life and to learn to live it as normally as possible.

As soon as I left the bank I went to a barber shop and had my hair cut short in the crew style, an adolescent affectation that would be useful at that time. I examined myself in a mirror and was satisfied that I no longer looked like any sort of Carleton. But to complete the picture I wanted I dressed from then on in cheap suntans, heavy brogans, a worker's blue shirt and the kind of short leather jacket worn by motorcycle riders. I looked then as if I belonged about the wharves.

Ginny was not at all pleased by my new appearance, as soon as she realized that it seemed to be permanent. In bed, one night, she told me, "I don't like it. You're trying too hard."

"To be what?"

"Like the others."

"Does it seem affected?"

"No, that isn't it. You're a perfect picture of a fisherman, or some kind of dockside worker. But it's too perfect, for you. You're not the kind to go for a haircut like that and cheap clothes of that sort." Then a new thought frightened her and she clung to me and gasped, "Oh, Tom, I'm sorry. I should have known. What has happened? Are the police getting closer?"

I was momentarily at a loss and asked, "What are you talking about?"

"You don't have to tell me. You really don't. I should have guessed right away. You're worried about being recognized, something has happened, so you're hiding behind those cheap clothes." Her fingers dug into my shoulders as she cried, "Maybe it would be better, to leave Monterey. I'll go with you. I don't care where. You can hide out somewhere else, where it's safer. Wouldn't that be better? You don't even have to work at anything. I can make enough for the two of us. Please don't be foolish, Tom."

That was the first offer I had ever had to be supported by a woman. The idea was even intriguing for a few minutes. I said, "Maybe you're right."

She sat up in bed and ran her fingertips along my cheek. "Of course I am. You're scared, or you wouldn't dress like that, and that scares me. We can leave right away, if you want."

"But in your kind of work we'd have to go to a large city and that wouldn't be so good."

"No, we don't. We can go to a small place. I can always get a job as an ordinary waitress, or working in a cannery, or anything like that. I wouldn't mind, Tom. Honestly I wouldn't. And you'd be safe."

I pulled her down in my arms and brushed my lips through her hair. "Thanks, Ginny. You're pretty wonderful. But it isn't necessary."

"If you're in danger, though—"

"I'm in no more danger here than I would be elsewhere."

"Honestly?"

"Yes."

"Then why—?"

"It's just one of those things. Dressing well, in the business I'm in, makes me a bit too conspicuous. I just decided to look like the rest of the gang."

Her fear gave way to exasperation. "But it isn't becoming!"

"Nevertheless," I laughed, "that's the way it's going to be. You'll just have to get used to it."

I held her closer and suddenly she giggled, "Now, Tom. Please. Oh, my darling—"

Ginny accepted the change with no further comment. With Gail, however, it was another matter. I ran into her on the street one day and, as it was the noon hour, asked her to have lunch with me. She frowned at my clothes and seemed a bit dubious, but went along with me to the Casa Munras. As soon as we had ordered, she also remarked on my change of costume.

"A bit sudden, isn't it?"

I nodded. "Mmmmmm."

"The *Rosita*'s at sea, so you aren't dressed for work. You look like a two-bit character who has never worn a suit in his life, but wants to show off to the boys in the pool room. Why?"

I tasted the soup when it arrived, then glanced across the table at her. "Maybe your friend Moore is right. Perhaps I have a bad record. I could even be hiding from the police."

"You could be doing anything, as far as I'm

concerned. But I don't think you have a record. Tom, just what is your past? Where are you really from? No one knows anything about you, including Matt."

"That's the way I like it."

She, too, appeared exasperated and snapped, "You just don't care to tell anyone."

"That's right. I like to be accepted full-blown, as I am this moment. I am not looking for approval as you are, understand, but merely acceptance."

She smiled coolly. "And it hasn't worked. Has it?"

"Not yet."

"It won't. You're much too distant and too arrogant, too, to be accepted by the people around you. You can't change your own nature."

"I think I can. At least, it's worth trying."

"Anyway," she pouted, "what do you mean by me looking for approval?"

"My dear, that is a constant anxiety of yours, that search for approval. You were fortunately given an abundance of beauty, but you nevertheless have a deep sense of insecurity. It probably comes from your early life, when your father was striving to get ahead. As he went up the ladder, your parents shoved you before them in the endeavor to make you better and superior to your friends. It's like the skin of a snake that has been shed but is still being dragged around. You're never quite sure of yourself. You're forced to seek approval and justification in the eyes of others. You're like a scullery maid invited to a grand banquet and terrified at the thought of using the wrong fork, making the wrong move, saying the wrong thing. Everything you do has to be approved by others."

She gave me an angry look and jabbed her fork viciously into a fillet of sole. The luncheon continued in silence. I glanced now and then at the sheer perfection of her hair, make-up and wardrobe. I wondered what she would be like if she decided, Oh, the devil with it, and allowed her natural beauty to shine forth without fuss and bother. It was not exactly a surprise, though I was perturbed, to realize that in such an event Gail would have more to offer than virtually any woman I had ever known.

Toward the end of the meal she cupped her chin in her hands, looked seriously at me and said, "Somehow—I don't know—maybe you are right, in a way. But do you really think that's the way I am?"

"I'm sure of it. However, I neither condemn or approve. In me you see the disinterested bystander. I am the last person in the world to judge the actions or motives of others."

A sly, little smile tugged at her lips. "But you aren't disinterested. You've given some time and thought to what I must be like. I enjoy that. You know—the other night—I'm sorry I was so obvious. I really did try hard to get you to make a play for me. Then I was going to be haughty and indignant, or at least laugh at you. Corny, wasn't it?"

We looked into each other's eyes and suddenly burst out laughing. That laughter was the first sign of some sort of rapport between us and I felt good about it, as if I had accomplished something.

But the next moment she was again serious. "You are a queer one," she said. "You know, I haven't forgotten the way that man was staring at you in the cocktail room of the Lodge. For a minute, at least, he was positive he knew you and there was something about it that startled him. I noticed, too, the way a lot of the staff around there thought they knew you at first. And that waitress who seated us— Who did she say she thought you were?"

I took a deep sip of coffee and mumbled, "I've forgotten. Obviously, I reminded them all of some free-spender who must hit the Lodge quite often."

She nodded and whispered, "Yes." Her eyes continued to hold mine, a growing idea in their depths.

I called for the check and broke up the luncheon as quickly as possible.

Gail had an engagement with Moore at his plant and had not brought her car downtown, so I drove her to the Moore-Ellsberg cannery on Cannery Row. But she had me stop the car a block from the cannery. Before getting out, she leaned toward me, as if we were conspirators, and whispered, "Be careful of Steve, Tom. He's really out for your hide. I don't understand why he feels so strongly about you—"

"I do. He knows that he amuses me. That drives him frantic. He doesn't consider himself a proper subject of amusement, so he has to retaliate. So far he hasn't been very successful."

"He has a lot of power. He'll find a way to get at you. Why don't you try to avoid him?"

"I can't. You see, he really does amuse me."

Gail's expression clouded. "Oh, don't be so damnably conceited. You can't fight a man like Steve. Just who do you think you are?"

"Someone who thinks it can be done."

"Oh, you—you're absolutely impossible."

She stepped out of the car, turned on her heel and disgustedly walked away. I watched her long legs and the so-feminine sway of her hips and again had to approve. She really had it.

I drove home feeling that I had had a pleasant time, but when I pulled up in front of the cottage my good spirits hit bottom with a thud. A sedan that had obviously been driven some distance was parked under the trees. The car was covered with dust and insects were smashed into the radiator grille and against the hood and windshield. A little man in a blue serge suit was seated behind the wheel reading a newspaper. He watched me get out of my car and walk toward the cottage. He hurried to get out of his automobile and joined me on the small porch.

"Mr. Howie?"

"Yes."

He took a business card from his pocket and handed it to me. "I'm Frank Kinnan from Los Angeles. Private investigator. I'd like a little talk with you, if you don't mind."

"What about? I don't owe anyone anything."

"This concerns a check you cashed a few days ago."

"Oh. That Carleton check?"

"Correct."

"Okay. Come on in."

He followed me into the living room, looked shrewdly about, then settled himself in a chair by the radio. I went into the kitchen for some beer and brought a bottle to Kinnan, which he accepted gratefully. I tossed my leather jacket over a chair and settled myself on the couch across the room. The palms of my hands were heavy with perspiration. I drank deeply out of the beer bottle and tried to get control of myself. Kinnan was the first link with my past. It would be easy for me to blunder.

I cautioned myself to talk as much like a fisherman as possible and said, "I've been worried about that check. At first I didn't think it was any good, but when I knew it was then the guy was dead."

Kinnan nodded his bald head, but offered no help. "I see."

"I kind of had a hunch it would bounce on me. I guess that's why you're here."

"Not at all. There is nothing wrong with the check."

I forced a smile of exaggerated relief and exclaimed, "Say, that's terrific! Then it's really good? Man, I can do a lot with that kind of dough. Got my eye on a nice little boat down here in the harbor."

"You're a fisherman, Mr. Howie?"

"Yeah. Been in the game most of my life. Sometimes it's lousy and sometimes pretty good. I can't complain."

"They didn't seem to know much about you at the Monterey Bank, but they did tell me you were in the fishing business." He sipped his beer, then leaned forward to say, "You see, when that check came through for clearance in the Carleton account some of the higher-ups in his organization thought it should be investigated. They'd like to know just how you got that check and why you hung onto it so long."

I said, "Hell's bells, mister, that's easy to explain. I met this Carleton guy when I was down south looking for a job. Don't he have a yacht down there?"

"I believe so."

"That's what he said. Me and him run into each other in a bar in Pedro. Got drinking together. Kind of a snotty character, if you really wanta know what I think about him, but an all-right Joe when it came to spending."

Kinnan attempted to hide a smile and failed. "He's been called a bastard by experts. But, just when was it you met him?"

I thought of the last time I had been to San Pedro prior to the accident and said, "Three days before he was killed."

He nodded, checked a small calendar in his wallet and wrote down the date. "I see."

"So we left this bar and went to a couple others and got oiled, then went up to my hotel room. Two other characters come along and we got a poker game going."

"The others were friends of yours?"

"Nope. I didn't know them. Just guys in a bar."

"Oh."

"Yeah, that's it. So this Carleton had maybe six hundred clams in cash and me and him cleaned out the other two guys and they pulled out."

"Then he was lucky?"

"In cards, yeah. But then he wanted to shoot craps with me. We bought some dice in a drugstore and went back to the room and shot craps all night. He didn't do so bad at first, but his luck changed. He started plunging and run out of cash. Well, sir, he had this here check for thirty-one thousand skins and wanted to draw on that. I couldn't see no profit in that—I thought it was strictly a phony—no one I knew ever had that kind of dough, but he swore up and down it was good and I figured, well, maybe I'd string along a while, anyways. So I did."

"And you won the whole check?"

I glared at him belligerently and shouted, "You're damned tootin' I did. Think I rolled him for it? Now, you look here, mister—"

"No, no. I didn't mean to imply that. I guess you were pretty lucky."

"Aw, it wasn't me so much. He clipped himself. The guy just didn't know how to figure the odds and every time he missed he plunged heavier than ever. He took himself. I just coasted along and won the works."

Kinnan looked off into space and nodded, picturing in his mind how it could have been. But then he asked, "Why didn't you cash it right away?"

I managed an expression of acute embarrassment. "Well, sir, I'll tell you. I never seen that much lettuce before in my life. Know what I mean? When I sobered up I didn't think it could be real. You see? It just couldn't be a slob of a fisherman like me with that kind of dough in my pocket."

Kinnan laughed. "I think anyone would feel the same way."

"Then you know how it is. So I stewed around like a guy with a bull by the tail and not knowing what to do about it and then I'm damned if I don't read that here this Carleton's got himself killed in an accident. Then I think the check's no good, after all. I mean, maybe it could be a good one, but with him dead it's no good. What I know about that sort of thing is nothing. Believe it or not, mister, I almost tore it up."

"No."

"It's the truth. But I hung onto it and a couple days ago I get thinking about it and a friend tells me why don't I deposit it and see what happens. You can't kill a man for trying and, anyways, I did win it fair and square. So I put it in the bank." I paused, then asked eagerly, "And you say it's all right?"

He finished his beer and got to his feet with a broad smile. "Sure, it's all right. As far as I know, the check has been honored. You'll probably have the money in your bank today or tomorrow. No one is interested in taking it away from you. The Carleton outfit won't miss it. They were just curious as to how you had come by it."

"Oh." Still pretending extreme eagerness, I said, "If you'd like to take down a statement, or something—"

"That isn't necessary. I'm satisfied with your story. Carleton was a heavy spender and he did gamble now and then."

I thought, Now and then? How little you know. But I said, "Any way I can help—"

"Oh, no. I'll turn in my report and that will be the end of it."

"Okay. Good. I can sure use the dough. By the way, was his body ever found?"

"No. Washed out to sea, I suppose."

"The guy sure had himself in a jackpot, all right. Imagine him losing his head and leaving that borrowed gun in that murdered doll's apartment. I guess it was just as well he clobbered himself."

He looked puzzled, but nodded and said, "Yes." He turned toward the door and I went with him, but there he paused and carefully appraised me. "You know, it's a funny thing, but you look a little like the late Carleton himself."

Ice was in my spine, but I forced a hearty laugh and slapped him on the back. "That's a lot of malarkey, chum. What I remember of that guy, he was plenty smooth."

"Yes, he was, at that. I didn't know him personally, but I used to see him around a good deal."

My heart was hammering wildly in the cage of my chest, but he suddenly smiled and shook hands and a moment later he was gone. Carleton, I thought, died with his leaving a non-existent body washed out to sea. And perhaps it was just as well.

I dropped weakly into a chair, feeling limp and exhausted and washed out. Having to face it finally as something definite and conclusive left me rather numb. Though she had lost her life, Bunny had achieved a victory of sorts, after all. Carleton was just as dead to the world and had paid with everything he possessed.

Thinking of Carleton in the third person was no longer so hard to do. It was becoming easier every day, as if the name had simply been that of an acquaintance I had known some time in my life. Now I could concentrate solely on myself as Tom Howie. My story had been accepted, the check was good, the gamble had paid off and I could really start living again without fear. But I did not feel as relieved as I should have been, or as exhilarated. Something was wrong.

When I realized what it was I tried to put it from

my mind as an impossibility. If, with my help, Matt cleaned up in the sardine game he would stand a better chance with Gail—and I resented the idea. But that was preposterous. It was more likely that I was again feeling the impulse to tread on dangerous ground by interfering. That I considered a rational idea and a sensible explanation, but yet . . .

CHAPTER TWELVE

Joseph Lagomarsino, the owner of the purse seiner *Rosita*, had retired from fishing after the second bad season and was living on the charter proceeds from the boat. I had a hunch that he would be willing to sell at a bargain price rather than gamble on the shares of another season. I talked it over with the cashier of the Monterey Bank, who agreed with me, but also mentioned that Steve Moore, too, was interested in the boat. I called on Lagomarsino at once.

The gnarled old fisherman assumed a reluctant attitude toward parting with the boat, but the hungry gleam in his eyes gave away the fact that he was more than eager to get rid of it. He mentioned that it would cost sixty thousand to duplicate the boat, but conceded that it was fairly old, that depreciation had written off a considerable portion of its value and, anyway, there were no longer purchasers for sardiners.

I offered twenty thousand and saw the muscles twitch at the corners of his mouth. The boat was probably worth more than that, but it was obvious that he would eventually accept that sum, or something close to it. He asked for thirty-two thousand. We argued back and forth a number of hours and finally got the price down to twenty-six thousand, splitting the difference. I was inclined to keep at him until the price was brought down to twenty, but amazingly found myself agreeing to the price of twenty-six. My God, I thought, maybe I'm not such a heel after all. But I decided to say nothing about it to Matt. He would never believe it.

We went together to the Monterey Bank the following day to make out the necessary papers of transfer of title. There I learned that the old man's equity in the boat was only fifteen thousand. The bank had been holding a note against it for eleven. I paid off Lagomarsino, then offered to pick up the bank note. The cashier looked sheepish and explained nervously that Steve Moore had bought the note from them at a discount the previous afternoon. I would have to get in touch with Moore to secure that note.

It took but a few minutes to drive to the cannery and walk to Moore's upstairs office facing over the water. He was seated behind his desk, looking toward me as I came in. He was smiling smugly, not at all surprised by my visit. I closed the door and became the surprised one. Gail Norton was seated in a chair on the other side of the door, so that I had not seen her as I came in. She gave me a startled glance and looked inquiringly toward Moore. He chuckled happily, laced his fingers together over the desk and nodded me into a chair facing him. He had the exact expression of a cat that has cornered a mouse.

"I suppose," he said, "you've heard about the boat."

"Yes."

"So now you figure I own the *Rosita* I'm politely going to give you the old bounce. If that's the way you're thinking," he paused to laugh, then continued, "you're absolutely right. Your charter expires in another month. And you won't get another boat. I've seen to that. There isn't an owner in the fleet who'd charter you a boat when I've told 'em not to." He rolled a fat cigar about in his mouth, touched a match to it and fairly beamed at me. "So now, my fine feathered friend, you're going to leave Monterey whether you like it or not—or starve: Got that?"

I restrained the impulse to laugh in his face and said, "But my understanding was that you've only picked up the bank note on the *Rosita*."

He waved an impatient hand before his face. "Just a detail. I can buy out old man Lagomarsino's equity any time I feel like it."

"I doubt that."

He grinned around the cigar. "Yeah? Any time, chum. All I gotta do is make an offer. You're on your way out, pal. One more month and you can start walking." He winked at Gail, then said, "On the other hand, I can be big about it, too. I can always use a spare janitor here at the cannery."

It was a pleasure for me to say, "I'm afraid you're a little behind time, Moore." I took the transfer of title from my wallet and placed it on the desk. "You see, I already own the *Rosita*. Furthermore, I'm here to pick up the note."

He stared at the transfer, the cigar drooping from

his mouth and his face an apoplectic red. It took him a long while to really believe what he was seeing. His eyes were riveted on the piece of paper, following it hungrily as I replaced it in my wallet. Then his eyes came up to mine and there was almost a killing rage in their beady depths.

I said, "The note, if you don't mind. I'm offering to pay it off in cash. You can't hold it."

He swallowed hard, licked his lips and mumbled, "I—I don't have it here. It's in the bank."

"All right. I'll meet you there at noon tomorrow and pick it up."

When I got up to leave he roared, "Where the hell'd you get that kind of money?"

"That's my business."

"Yeah? I'm making it mine, too. There's something plenty phony about you. I know how you were picked up in San Pedro. Tony told me all about it. You don't rate that kind of dough. And I know you ain't made it in shark."

"I print it myself."

"Oh, yeah, wise guy? Look, chum; I warned you before to clear out. I ain't kidding. Owning the *Rosita*'ll do you no good. You won't be able to sell a sardine anywhere on Cannery Row. All I gotta do is pass the word. Understand? Then where'll you be?"

"Moore," I said, "you're a very laughable and yet a sad sort of character, too. Stupid. I know the situation with the canners here. You're all at each other's throats. Any sardines I get will be bought gladly and with great joy by any one of your competitors. So why don't you just relax and try to live with me? I'm really pretty cute when you get to know me." I smiled at him and could not resist saying, "Besides, we have a few things in common. We could have a sort of gentlemen's agreement to split dates with Gail—"

He turned on her and asked savagely, "You been seeing this character again?"

She leaned toward us and said anxiously, "Please, Steve. And Tom—"

"I asked you not to see him again. Now, didn't I ask you that, or didn't I?" He slumped back in his chair and clamped his teeth down on the ragged cigar. His beady little eyes jumped back and forth between us, his small brain evidently arriving at the conclusion that we were seeing a great deal of each other. Then a cold smile pulled at his lips. "Not anymore," he said. "Not from now on. You see, chum, me and Gail are gonna get married. So I'm telling you to stay away and she'll be telling you to stay away—or else."

I turned away from him to watch Gail. She had caught her breath and was staring fixedly at Moore. He gave her an almost imperceptible nod. She continued staring at him, her expression that of a woman engaged in cold and rapid calculation, balancing the revulsion she could hardly help feeling against the recovery of her fortunes with Moore at the helm. It was an odd way to receive a proposal, but it was nevertheless the goal she had been striving to attain. She tried to look at me, but her eyes slid away. Her lips thinned to a firm line as she returned Moore's nod.

I felt irritated and disgusted and, somehow, defeated. I had to get away from the two of them. I suppose my precipitate exit was rather childish, but that could not be helped. If I had stayed a moment longer I would have gone around the desk after Moore. So I left. But even as I went out I felt a wild wave of excitement beginning to mount. The same old story. Where Gail was concerned, the odds of danger were now increased considerably.

I busied myself with the sardine problem and there came up against a few hard facts of which I had not been aware. I had thought the purse seine net would be a minor expense, but to my dismay and the upsetting of all my calculations, I had to pay fourteen thousand dollars for one and that one was second-hand. Repairing it and putting it in fishing condition cost more. Then there was the problem of a turntable for the net. The *Rosita's* original turntable had been sitting in a vacant lot for almost three years and was in bad shape. Repairing that came high. The old brailing net, too, was no longer any good. I had to buy another. When I finished I was almost broke.

But long before then I had known I could not pick up the note Moore held on the *Rosita* and had had to notify the bank to that effect. That note in Moore's pocket became a source of constant worry. I could only hope that Matt was having luck at sea.

The day before Matt returned I was sitting at the counter of Slats' Fish Grotto on the wharf, enjoying a shrimp cocktail and some beer, when Gail suddenly slid onto the stool at my side. She smiled at me nervously and ordered a crab cocktail with plenty of hot sauce. When I glanced at the ostentatious diamond ring on her left hand she tried to hide it.

"Too big," I said. "You need a newspaper to hide that, or a cannery."

She blushed and shifted uneasily on the stool. "Do you really think it's too big?"

"Not if you intend hocking it at some future date."

"Well, it's kind of yellow—"

I had to smile. "For your information, my dear, some of the world's most expensive diamonds are yellow. Moore isn't so stupid, after all."

"Really?" She looked relieved.

"But aren't you taking a chance being seen with me? Moore may take that ring back and then you'll have to start all over again looking for someone else with money."

She looked angry, but asked softly, "You despise me, don't you?"

"Not at all. I admire you. You must have tremendous courage to think of going to bed with a slob like Moore."

She shuddered. "Please, Tom. He isn't so bad. Really." She turned closer to me and her lips were again thin and grim with resolution. She stared off into space as she said, "I've tried everything, every possible avenue, but Steve is the only man I know who can pull the Norton Cannery out of the red. That I must have."

"How about Matt?"

"He can do it, too, but he won't. So—"

"Sure. You know, Gail, the best thing that could happen to you would be to lose that damned cannery and the house you're in and whatever else you have and let down your hair and start over again at scratch with someone like Matt."

An odd little smile lighted her eyes as she whispered,

"Or someone like you?"

I stared into her eyes, but could not read the meaning of her words. Obviously, too, she was going to allow me to interpret them in any way I pleased. She shoved the cocktail aside and hastily got up from the stool to leave. I reached for her arm, but she twisted away and hurried out of the restaurant. I was tempted to go after her, but sank back to the stool instead. It was no good. I did not know my own mind, regardless of what her attitude toward me may have been. I had to let her go.

I turned my attention back to the beer and drank steadily all afternoon. That was something I knew how to do well.

CHAPTER THIRTEEN

Matt and the crew returned to harbor a few days before the official opening of the sardine season with a well-stocked hold of shark liver cans. I went down to the wharf to meet them and shook hands all around. All except Tony were glad to see me. It was evident he resented the fact that I would share in the catch as usual even though I had not been aboard. He was surly and did not even bother to say hello.

I helped them unload the cans and placed them on a refrigerated truck going to San Francisco for vitamin A analysis, then invited the whole crew out for drinks. We went to a bar and I listened to the accounts of the voyage. Nothing had gone wrong, the weather had been fair, the long drift net had worked perfectly and they had run into one soup-fin school after another. Listening to them and sharing vicariously in their excitements and triumphs and picturing how it had been I had difficulty remembering that I had ever been anything but a fisherman. I felt some pride, too, in their accomplishments, even as a bench-warming member of the team.

The crew scattered and big Matt and I were left alone. His eyes were red from lack of sleep, there were deep tired lines about his mouth, his hands were burnt and scarred from creosote on the nets and his ragged, smelling clothes indicated hard work to the limits of a man's ability. But his powerful shoulders were squared and a small boy eagerness was burning in his sea blue eyes. I felt more sudden affection for him at that moment than I had ever felt for anyone in my life. Matt was all man, a giant among giants.

"The way I figure it," he said, "after deducting costs, and if the market still holds the way it was when I left—"

"It does. I've been checking."

"Good. Then you and I stand to split about cighty-five hundred between us. Okay?" He grinned.

"Great. We can use it. I've been busy too—"

"Save it. Let's go to your place and talk. But first I have to get out of these clothes."

We went to Matt's room and I waited while he splashed about in a tub like a sea lion and roared out a selection from some operetta considerably off key. When he had changed to clean clothes we went to my cottage and relaxed. Matt had a couple of straight shots to tickle his tongue and wash the salt out of his throat, then took his time over a long, cool one.

He squinted at me over his glass and asked, "Seen Gail?"

"A few times. Still thinking of her in the same way, Matt?"

"I don't change my mind easily."

"Then I'm sorry I have to be the one to tell you. The little girl has made the grade, Matt. She's engaged to Steve Moore."

Matt looked away from me and stared out the window, in his eyes the sea and the nets and the back-breaking labor he had put in. I could almost see the knife twisting within his chest and the steady drip of blood from his heart. But when he looked back at me his face was a mask.

"They're not married yet."

"No."

He lifted his drink in a huge paw and swallowed a large portion of it. "Good. Now, then, about you and me busting into sardines. It's going to be a good season. Every night I saw schools scattered all over the ocean. We tracked some of them and measured their size with the fathometer. They're running heavy. Everyone around here thinks it's going to be lousy again, but I know better. All we have to do is get in and we'll hit it big." He gave me a sharp glance. "Anything on your mind?"

I smiled. "Plenty."

"I figured so. Between the two of us—if you haven't been doing any spending—we should have around twenty thousand dollars. That's why I'm riding with you. Together we may be able to break the ice, though it's mighty damned thick."

"The ice," I said, feeling much like Santa Claus, "is already broken." I leaned forward and must have grinned at him like a schoolboy. "You and I are already in business, Matt. I've bought the *Rosita*, a net, the works. You can start operating any time the season opens."

He put his glass slowly aside, his eyes never leaving my face. "Let's have it. Start from the beginning."

I told him the whole story, except for one detail. I would not tell him where I had acquired the check, or from whom, saying merely that I had it and that was that. He felt that I was lying and I could hardly blame him. In his code a man was either worth that kind of money, which, to him, I was not, or he had somewhere come by it dishonestly.

"Well," he said, "you've managed to chisel it somewhere. I'm damned if I can figure it out, or you either, but it's no skin off my nose. But where do I fit in the picture? You don't really need me, you know. You can hire a good skipper."

"We started together, or at least I started with you. Let's keep it that way. Now, I have put out a lot of money and I'm worried about that note Moore holds. So let's do it this way: You pay me ten thousand cash and give me sixty day notes for the balance, with options to protect you, and we'll sign partnership papers. Fair enough for you?"

"Fair?" he snorted. "Geez!" He got out of his chair and paced slowly up and down the room for a while, then paused facing me. "Look, Tom, there isn't a boat owner in Monterey who would offer me a deal like that. For ten thousand bucks and some notes—"

"You have to amortize them."

"Nevertheless, you've bought yourself a whip and you're not using it. That doesn't fit my picture of you. Frankly, I'm suspicious of every move you make. Now, why are you doing it?"

The pride I had been feeling in what I had accomplished, at considerable risk, began to fade before his estimate of me. Why had I done it? Friendship? Affection? Purely liking for the big man? Possibly I, too, was seeking approval, Matt's approval. I had no ready answer.

I shrugged and said dully, "I don't know. But, what the hell, if you think there's a catch somewhere—"

"Hey, wait a minute. I'm grabbing it. Understand? You got yourself a partner. All I hope is that your nose is clean. Now, let's get down to business."

We went to an attorney, worked out the details and made out all the necessary papers. It was no sooner accomplished than I realized I had lost my enthusiasm for the project. I had been no better than Gail. I had been looking for Matt's ungrudging approval and had received suspicion instead. I had carried a fairly difficult project through to a successful conclusion and my pride in it was reduced to nothing.

Yet, I thought, I had learned something from it, and from Gail. We all searched for approval in some form or other. As Carleton, I had thought I was above that sort of thing, so isolated on my mountain top that I had not even to consider it, but as Tom Howie I had subconsciously sought the approval of others. The same person, but differing circumstances. It came as a shock to realize that even as Carleton, or anyone, approval was necessary and the lack of it had contributed to my imbalance. I had been fighting that strange vacuum all my life.

I wanted to think the problem through, to cut through another layer of gold-encrusted hide, so avoided Matt the next few days. That was easy, as he was busy. He had enrolled the two of us in the owners' association and was battling in company with them against the canners over the price per ton to be paid for sardines. The owners were holding out for forty dollars and the canners, naturally, wanted to pay much less. The arguments went on day and night.

I wandered about the wharves and gave the crew a hand now and then in converting the *Rosita* back to a purse seiner, but most of my time was spent with Ginny. The weather was good, with sunny, warm days, so every noon we drove to Carmel and lay in the sun on the salt-white beach. I was feeling indolent and rather at odds with myself and surroundings, so was not much of a conversationalist. Ginny, however, chattered away like a magpie on our beach excursions. In her low, throaty voice, lying close by my side and pouring sand on my chest, she would express herself on every topic that came to her mind.

One day, right after I had been in swimming, she said dreamily, "It's funny, Tom, but I guess I don't have an ambitious bone in my body."

"How about your whirl in Hollywood?"

She shrugged. "Oh, that. That was just something everyone seemed to think I should do. I got interested, maybe even a little excited, but I wasn't really thinking ahead. Now that I think of it I realize that if I had really been ambitious I wouldn't have minded crawling from one casting couch to another. But Gail, now—"

"Uh-huh."

"I'm not being catty. Honest. It's true, though. In the same spot I was in, Gail would have weighed her chances and gone on from couch to couch to wind up a star. If that was what she wanted she wouldn't have minded following any means to get it. You know. Like with Steve. It's the same thing, really."

"I guess. But do you just intend coasting through life and letting the future take care of itself?"

She eased herself to her back and clasped her hands behind her head, pulling taut the twin perfection of her breasts. I knew every detail of her lovely body by that time, but it continued to excite me as much as it had in the beginning, perhaps even more so. I doubted if one could really ever "get used" to a body such as Ginny's.

"Well," she answered, "sometimes I do think about the future, a little. But I'm lazy, you see. I don't care to work very hard to do something about it."

"How about glamour, wealth, prestige, power?"

"For me? Nonsense. Maybe I could have got all that in Hollywood, but it didn't happen and I don't much care." She laughed and said, "If it had happened I would have been faced with a lot of hard work and I don't care much for that."

I turned on an elbow to watch her expression and asked, "How about marriage?"

Her features tightened for a moment with a twinge

of pain, then relaxed. She gave me a light smile and rubbed her fingertips along my cheek. "When you mention marriage, Tommy, you're not thinking of us. You're thinking of me and someone else. I've gotten to know you pretty well now."

"You could be wrong."

She closed her eyes against the sun and shook her head. "No. Wherever you've come from your background has been different than mine. And if you ever get out of this trouble you're in, whatever it is, you'll marry someone out of that same background. I know how you are. You're not in love with me and I like the way you don't pretend you are. I'm just something nice to have around right now, to make love to, to go to bed with, to lie on the beach like this—but not a wife."

I started to protest, but she said, "Please. We've been honest all along. Let's keep it that way. I'm enjoying myself the way things are. I don't say I wouldn't like them to be different, but—well—this is how it is."

She was silent for a long time, but just as we were about to leave she said, "One of these days you'll be gone. And I don't think that's so far off."

"Why do you say that?"

"Oh, because of little things you do lately. You've been working like a beaver on this sardine business, but all of a sudden, now that everything seems to be sewed up, you don't have the interest you had. Then there's your feeling about Matt. He's let you down, some way or other. All sorts of little things. The way you stare off into space most of the time, so damned preoccupied I could scream at you. But the big thing is you're not so nervous and worried anymore."

That was important to know. I asked, "You're sure of that?"

"Oh, yes. You've changed a lot recently. You're not so belligerent, or nasty, or arrogant, or—or— Well," she laughed, "I'd say you're getting kind of normal. That's why I think you'll lose interest around here and take off any time."

I thought of it and shook my head. "You have it in reverse, Ginny. Suppose you were told by a doctor that you were about to die, or, at best, that life would be a form of lingering death. That would be a terrible cloud to live under. But suppose that cloud blew away and, though it would be impossible to ever return to the status quo, now you could look ahead and start living again."

She took it all wrong, of course, and gasped, "You thought you were suffering from some disease?"

"No, no, darling. It's purely hypothetical, but somewhat similar to what I've been going through."

"And that cloud has blown over?"

"In a way, yes. The cloud that was my past has blown away. It's a thing dead and buried. There's just Tom Howie left and a future to take care of. But I am not taking off, or going anywhere. My future is right here. I have lost a lot, more than you will ever know, yet I have been fortunate, too. Sheer luck has landed me on my feet. I intend staying that way."

She was puzzled and silent for some time, then said, "But you don't really belong in this atmosphere."

"I belong where I have found myself. I like it. I enjoy the hard work and the sea and the fishing and the people who have become my friends, or who have just casually accepted me. It's like being born all over again. In fact, this is even hard for me to believe. I don't think I would trade it for my past even if I could."

"That's news to me. I had it figured out differently." Then tired lines appeared at the corners of her mouth as she said wearily, "We still come back to what you asked me before—marriage, with someone else. That I have to think about."

"How will that go?"

"I don't know. Here it wouldn't be good. Here I have the reputation of being a pushover. So help me God, Tommy, never in my life have I ever done anything to earn a reputation like that. To think of anyone touching me I wasn't in love with would drive me crazy. I couldn't even allow myself to be petted like the other girls. Just the idea gave me cold shivers. So I guess that made all my dates angry and some of them bragged about sleeping with me and got themselves believed because I look that way, anyway, and that started it. Then one time there was a dirty, filthy-minded Peeping Tom with a long-range camera—"

I said gently, "I know. I've heard all about it. Matt told me the full story."

"Thank God, he was the one to tell you. Well, you can imagine what that did. So every time I walk down the street half the men in town see me in the nude and they're not thinking of me as the little woman sitting at home by the fireside. Like Steve Moore. He's offered me practically everything he has, but no ring. He's afraid that if he married me—God, what a horrible idea! All his friends would be secretly laughing at him. You see how it would be?" She paused, bit at her lower lip, then continued, "No, this isn't the town. I'll have to go somewhere else, maybe San Francisco, anywhere."

"And how will that be?"

"That," she whispered, "I'll find out when the time comes." She turned into my arms and held me tightly. "Meanwhile, Tommy, love me as much as you can."

There was nothing I could say to her. Quite aside from not knowing the state of my own emotions, I was in no position to talk marriage with anyone. My past was not yet that dead.

In fact, my past came suddenly back to life early that evening, after Ginny had gone to work. I was leaning in front of Slats' Grotto on the wharf, idly smoking a cigarette and watching the people stroll by, when I sensed that I was being watched. I felt that someone, a specific person, had his eyes constantly upon me. But it was hard to single out one person amongst so many, as at that time of year there were crowds of tourists wandering about the wharf. At last, however, I discovered him.

He was a middle-aged man with thin, graying hair, pursy lips and watery eyes and the humble bearing of a Caspar Milquetoast. He wandered about the stalls and fish markets and curio shops, but every time he moved, every turn he made, his eyes swept toward me and then slid away. But when I had discovered him and was sure that he was the cause of my uneasy feeling I felt relief rather than anxiety. He was such a harmless, unobtrusive little person.

It was not until the next evening, when I again saw him on the wharf, that I became aware of something familiar about him. He was so much like so many millions of other people that it was almost impossible to sort him out of the images in my mind. But I finally knew him. Mr. Milquetoast was the cashier of a bank I controlled in Beverly Hills where I kept my personal accounts. I had seen him and spoken to him and occasionally talked over minor financial matters with him at least once a week for ten or twelve years. He had never impressed me as being other than a fixture of the bank and I don't believe I had ever given him a second thought, but his identity was not in doubt.

I felt as if I had been slugged with a baseball bat and saw all of my plans burning to ashes. Frank Kinnan, the investigator, had evidently not believed my story and had probably been more than a little bemused by my resemblance to the supposedly dead Carleton. He could not have chosen a better man than the cashier to come up to Monterey to look me over. The odds were that I would not have noticed him, yet he would know me well enough and have ample leisure to appraise me. He was obviously not yet positive of my identity, as he would otherwise not still be watching me, yet, by the same token, he was probably not sure that I was not Carleton.

Fear clutched at my stomach and I thought instantly of flight, but as quickly ruled that out. I had to know. I had to be sure. It took every ounce of will to force myself into action, but I managed to cross the wharf and tap the man on the shoulder. He stared at me as if I had hit him with my fist.

"Mister," I said, "I don't know who the hell you are, but you're beginning to get in my hair. For the last couple days I've noticed you watching me. Do I owe you a bill, or something?"

He was nervous and also, oddly enough, seemed embarrassed. "I'm sorry," he mumbled, "but you are right. I have been watching you. You're Mr. Howie, aren't you?"

"That's right, chum."

"Yes. So I've been told." He tugged at his collar, stretched his scrawny neck, then said, "Well, sir, it's a strange story. Are you by any chance acquainted with the name of George Finley, the steel man?"

"Never heard of him."

"I see. Yes. Well, Mr. Finley lives in Bel Air, down in Los Angeles, and keeps his account in the bank where I am cashier. Not long ago he came in the bank in a very agitated frame of mind. He seemed to think he had seen a dead man."

"When you said strange you weren't kidding."

"No. So he asked me to see for myself. You, sir, are that dead man."

I felt a cold chill in my spine, but snorted, "Oh, now, wait a minute. Are you sure you're not drunk?"

He giggled and replied, "I am cold sober. But that is the story. That is why I have been watching you. The dead man, by the way, was T. Howard Carleton, owner of the bank where I work. And, you know, you do look like him."

"Yeah?"

"Yes, you do. Same physique, high coloring, black hair, eyes and—if you don't mind my saying so—the same arrogant manner in the way you walk and carry yourself. But there, of course, the similarities end."

I licked a tongue over dried lips and said, "So I don't look like him."

"Well, you do and you don't. I mean to say, there is a striking resemblance, truly amazing, and I can well understand why Mr. Finley was so startled. I, however, have had a chance to observe you at greater length. There are too many other differences. Perhaps, with the help of a good make-up artist and a few—well— physical changes about the face, you could be made to look like the late Mr. Carleton, but otherwise, on any sort of close inspection, you could never really be mistaken for him."

I began to breathe easier and even managed to laugh. "It's always nice to know I ain't a dead man."

He smiled at me sheepishly. "I am sorry if I have disturbed you. But Mr. Finley was so upset and I was due for a little vacation, anyway. Besides, it was pretty much of an adventure, you know." He looked sad as he said wistfully, "I rather hated to tell Mr. Finley he was wrong."

"So you've already told him that?"

"Oh, yes. I've been watching you for the past four days. So I telephoned Mr. Finley last evening and told him that he could forget the whole matter. He was vastly relieved."

"Yeah. So am I."

But it went far deeper than simple relief. It seemed to be the last assurance I needed that I was safe. Kinnan, after all, had believed my story and was apparently no longer interested in me. Now two others were added to the list of three who knew of the resemblance between Howie and Carleton, yet were convinced they were not one and the same person. The indication was clear that if anyone else out of my past should come across me and remark on the resemblance the end result would yet be the same.

It was comforting to know and I was naturally glad that I had kept my head long enough to learn that I was even safer than I had realized. I bought a bottle and drove home at dusk to enjoy a little solo celebration. Now, perhaps, I could think of Ginny, or even Gail, from a different perspective.

I had just settled myself with a tall glass when the doorbell rang. I opened the door to face Gail standing on the porch.

"I saw your car," she said, "so I thought—well—"

"Come in."

I stepped aside to let her in and she, typically the woman, had to wander about and inspect everything and comment on how "neat" and "cozy" the place was, obviously surprised that a bachelor lived in anything but a pig pen. I noticed, also, that she did not miss the little touches Ginny had contributed. She finally settled in a chair, crossed long, slim legs and lit a cigarette. I offered her a drink, but she shook her head. There was something about her appearance that puzzled and disturbed me, but I could not figure it out for the moment, so I tried to forget it.

When I mixed a highball for myself and dropped onto the couch opposite her, she smiled and said, "Of course, you knew I was lying. I wasn't just passing by. I wanted to see you."

"I'm glad of that."

She gave me a level, searching look. "Are you?"

"Certainly. You're more satisfying than a beautiful painting."

"And about as desirable?" She waited, but as I had nothing to say she leaned forward and said, "Tom, I understand you and Matt are all set for the pilchard season. Steve has been talking about it a great deal. He likes Matt, you know. In fact, I think he's a little afraid of him, but he isn't going to let that get in the way of his spite for you."

"Is that what you came to see me about?"

"Partly. Do you think I am being disloyal? Maybe I am. But I don't like the idea of a man deliberately harming someone that I—well—another person just because of petty spite. I don't want it to happen."

"There isn't much Moore can do to me—not anymore."

"But there," is she insisted. "The canners are competitors, yes, but they do hang together on some matters. They have their organization, too, you know. And Steve is spreading the word that you have a suspicious past, that no organization will bond you and that any canner who does business with you would be risking litigation at the least. I really doubt very much that you and Matt will be able to make any contracts on Cannery Row."

I thought it over, but as Carleton, not Howie. "It's all right," I said. "Matt will be able to work it without me."

She frowned and stared at me curiously. "How do you mean that?"

"I'm clearing out. You see, Gail, Moore is right in a way. My past is catching up with me, though not quite in the way he thinks. So I'm leaving."

She looked actually distressed and whispered tensely, "Oh, no. You can't do that."

It was my turn to be curious. "You sound as if you didn't want me to go."

Her eyes slid away from mine to hide an anxious expression in their depths. I wondered what could be wrong with her. She was achieving all she wanted and should not have cared whether I remained or disappeared in a puff of smoke. But my curiosity on that subject died as I suddenly realized what was different about her appearance. Gail's hair was not as precisely made up as I was used to seeing it. It was still beautiful, even more so, but not so ostentatiously. It had been combed loosely and was hanging about her shoulders in a softer manner. Her make-up, too, was not as hard or as brilliant as it had been, but was also in a softer mood. And there was something just slightly careless about her dress, really more becoming. Gail, in other words, was no longer thinking exclusively of Gail. There were obviously other problems on her mind that no longer allowed the same time devoted to self.

She said crossly, "I didn't think you were the kind who would run out on Matt."

"He thinks I am."

"But I don't."

"Anyway, he won't be hurt. We're all set up to operate. He can do that better without me. Moore won't get in his way without me around. He'll think he's achieved some sort of victory and Matt will have no trouble doing business on Cannery Row."

She shook her head in disagreement. "Matt needs you to get on his feet. He's too direct. You're devious. On the other hand," she sighed, "you may be right. There is a lot you don't know about Matt. Some ways, he is a great deal like Steve." I laughed and started to protest, but she shook her head and said stubbornly, "He is. Matt is more scrupulous than Steve, he is much more of a man and he has a finer code of ethics, but there are soft spots not so ethical. He keeps his own hands fairly clean, but he doesn't mind clasping dirtier hands if it serves his purpose."

There was something in her statement that suddenly opened a door in my mind. I thought of the manner in which I had bypassed Oka Halversen. Matt had not liked it, but he had gone along with me. He was also quite sure that I had pulled something raw in the matter of securing the *Rosita*, but again he had gone along with me.

Gail watched me closely, evidently following the direction of my thoughts. She added, "He's a ruthless man, Tom. He has too much of the arrogance of the big man. Believe me, if you ever got in his way, and it served his ends to do so, he would think nothing whatever of stepping on you. I like him in spite of that part of his nature, but that is the way he is." She smiled nervously and said, "Now I seem to be agreeing with you that it is better to leave him. I really don't mean it that way."

I asked with exasperation, "Then just what the devil do you mean?"

She shrugged her shoulders in a little gesture of helplessness. "I don't know." Her eyes slid away from mine and then she stood up, turning away from me. "Maybe it was a stupid idea to drop by, after all."

I stared at her, wondering, not quite believing an idea that had crept into my mind, then said softly, "Gail, come over here."

Her body tensed. She stood there rigidly for a long moment, then her eyelids fluttered and slowly she turned to face me. Her elbows were pressed in tight at her waist, her hands flat at her sides, fingers digging into flesh. She came toward me wide-eyed, jerkily, like a sleepwalker, or one fighting a tremendous emotional conflict. She stopped before me and pressed her flat stomach against my cheek and I could feel the trembling of her body. Her hands raised slowly and rested on my shoulders, gripping hard; her nails digging in.

I heard her catch her breath sharply, then she lowered herself tensely onto the couch at my side. Her eyes stared widely into mine, then suddenly she melted with an almost inaudible gasp and all the tension was gone and her lips were crushed hungrily against mine. It was as if a dam had broken, releasing the pent-up tension of years. Her body was almost burning and there was perspiration gathering on her forehead.

But I looked beyond her and could see Ginny dressing in the bedroom, or sweeping the floor, or working in the kitchen, or tuning the radio and humming softly and contentedly with the dance music. Gail was literally giving herself to me and desire for her was indeed powerful, but the atmosphere Ginny had created in the little cottage was much stronger.

I felt like a damned fool and probably looked like one, but I gently loosened Gail's arms and pushed her away. It was obvious that she was being rejected and I thought she would be either humiliated or hysterically angry, but after staring at me for a moment she seemed to be amused instead.

"Ginny," she whispered.

"I'm sorry, Gail."

"You're acting like a husband who doesn't wish to foul his wife's nest."

"Maybe that's it. I'm sorry."

She got to her feet and pulled down her skirt almost primly. "My God," she said, "what a situation. I didn't really mean this to happen and yet I suppose I did mean it and I feel like a fool." She glanced toward the open door to the bedroom, then looked back at me, that light of amusement still in her eyes.

She leaned over to pick up her purse from the couch and her full breasts brushed by my eyes. I had to grip the edge of the couch hard to keep my hands where they belonged, feeling more of a damned fool than ever. She straightened with a throaty little laugh, spun away from me and went into the kitchen. She arranged her clothes quickly, fixed her hair and returned to the living room.

She looked down at me and asked, "Ginny makes the difference?"

"I'm afraid so."

"I guess she would. She's made no attempt to hide her affair with you, you know. Practically everyone knows about it. Not that I blame you, you understand. I—well—I suppose any man would be intrigued by a sex-machine such as Ginny." She paused, bit her lip, then said, "It's just as well. I would have felt like a tramp, too."

The blood was still pounding too fiercely in my temples for me to become angry, but I said, "I don't like that. Ginny is no tramp."

"Oh, for God's sake," she cried, "don't be a complete fool. Don't blind yourself to the facts. I honestly hate to say it about my own cousin, but she is no good and never has been."

Rejection, I thought, was beginning to burn, after all. I said, "Let's forget Ginny."

"That's for you to do. And when you do—" She smiled, turned quickly away and went out the door.

I went out to the porch and saw her disappear in the dark toward her car. I waited until the engine started and the headlights went on and then vanished down the street. I walked slowly back into the house thinking of her last words and the virtual promise they contained. If I could erase Ginny from my mind and affections, then Gail would be waiting. That seemed to be it.

CHAPTER FOURTEEN

Negotiations between the boat owners and the canners dragged on after the official opening of the season, but the boats remained in harbor. Matt was not sure how long it would be before we could go fishing, so advised me to hang on to whatever cash I had instead of paying off Moore's note. We might need the money if the deadlock lasted too long. I would rather have paid the note, but there was really nothing pressing about it, so I let it go.

Then Matt came to my cottage one evening with the good news that the canners were anxious to get their plants operating. "This deadlock," he explained, "is no better for them than it is for us. They've been having a bad time, too, the last few seasons, and are in a pretty shaky position. Even Steve Moore is heavily in debt."

"The wonder boy himself?"

"God, yes." He poured a slug of raw whisky down his throat, followed it with a chaser and said, "Eighty percent of his plant is owned by the banks. Which reminds me. Your name is mud on Cannery Row. I'm having a hell of a time trying to get contracts with one of the outfits. My reputation is clean, but not yours. They're afraid of you. We may have to wind up doing business with one of the outfits at Moss Landing up the bay. And I'm not even too sure about that."

I said casually, "Looks like I'm not doing you any good."

He paced the floor restlessly and growled, "You're damned right you're not. I was wondering—" He paused to face me and punched a finger in my chest. "Look, Tom, suppose you drop out. What I mean, keep your interests exactly as they are, but drop out of active participation in the fishing. I can run the works without you. If we do that I can square it with the canners and get contracts. How would that be with you?"

I was staggered by the proposal and snapped back, "No damned good and you know it. I'd rather lose the works than back down before Moore."

"Listen," he barked, "I'm in this too, you know. I'm thinking strictly of Matt Radovich. Now, if you'd just sit back—"

"No dice. I'm going out with that fleet and get sardines even if they have to be dumped on the beach."

"What the hell brews with you and Steve, anyway?"

"Natural, inborn antagonism. And Gail got mixed up in it somewhere."

Matt's face clouded like a black thunderhead. "What has she to do with it?"

"Well, Moore didn't like the idea of me taking her out. I think I was the added incentive for him to become engaged to her. Since then it has probably become worse." I watched Matt's granite expression and felt the old urge to nudge at danger. "You see, Matt, he probably thinks Gail is more than a little interested in me, perhaps even in love. If he didn't already dislike me, he would at least hate me for that."

A hard smile was etched on Matt's thin lips. "I doubt if he is concerned about that."

"But why not?" I paused a moment, then said pointedly, "There could be something to it."

Matt moved swiftly across the room, grabbed my shirt in a big fist and lifted me to my feet. His face was contorted in an ugly grimace within a few inches of my own. "Listen, you bastard, I don't like that sort of chatter. I told you once before to stay away from Gail—"

"And what did I say about it?"

He shoved me away and I fell back in the chair. He stood there a moment looking down at me, his face twisted with hate and frustration, then turned on his heel and left the house. He slammed the door so hard it rocked the cottage. I thought, a cheap victory, and didn't like it. I had no idea then that I had suffered defeat rather than victory. I learned that the next day.

Matt telephoned in the morning, said that the deadlock would be broken that day and asked me to get the boat ready for the sea. He would be too busy. Ginny went down to the wharf with me, almost as excited as I, as I rounded up the crew. We had hired six other men in addition to Tony, Pete and Johnson, all of them good purse seiners. Tony was a hothead, with no love lost for me, but he had an air of authority about him, so I delegated him to take care of the stores and handle the crew. I was so green that without Matt around I didn't know what to do, anyway.

In the midst of all the activity, Ginny asked the sixty-four-dollar question; "Even if you get sardines, who are you going to sell them to?"

That had to be answered, so I took her uptown with me and called on an attorney suggested by the Monterey Bank. We looked up the laws concerning restraint of trade, then the attorney telephoned the manager of one of the biggest canneries, Holbrook and Stevens. Within two minutes the manager was in water beyond his depth and in another minute Holbrook was on the phone. Holbrook admitted that he knew who I was and complained that his information concerning Tom Howie was all bad. But when the attorney got through explaining the meaning of restraint of trade to him he reluctantly agreed to accept whatever haul the *Rosita* brought in. That was all I needed. Moore's campaign had collapsed.

Ginny wanted to stay with me and watch the fleet sail that night, if it did go out, but I argued her out of that and walked her toward the Las Olas. "You'd just be in the way, darling. I have too much work to do."

She nodded glumly. "It's all right."

She had nothing more to say and walked listlessly at my side until we reached the hotel. I was preoccupied with my own thoughts, but finally noticed her silence. "Anything wrong?" I asked.

She fumbled in her purse, took out a package of cigarettes and lit one. She leaned back against the hotel entrance, her eyes fixed on some object across the street. She said huskily, "I have a feeling this is the night."

"The night for what?"

"Where you and I go our separate ways."

"But that's nonsense."

"Is it?" Her dark eyes turned slowly to meet mine as she said nervously, "It's more than a feeling. In a barroom, you know, you hear a lot of talk. I've heard a lot about you and—and Gail."

"Why Gail? Why not anyone else? I've seen very little of her."

"Maybe that's all it takes. Look, Tommy; I know about you. I've said it before and I'll say it again. Maybe you're just a fisherman now and maybe you were practically a bum when Matt picked you up, but you have the same outlook of the upper classes. At some time or other you've really had it. I don't have that outlook. I don't belong in that class. But Gail thinks she does and I guess you do, too."

"Look here—"

"No, wait. I've been watching this coming. And lately, since about a week ago, I've been practicing on how to forget you in a hurry."

I was puzzled and asked, "Why the reference to a week ago? I don't understand."

"You had Gail at your cottage that evening. I knew it when I joined you there later. I know the perfume she uses." She paused, then said heatedly, "She wanted me to know she had been there. She left her lipstick brush on the kitchen sink and a handkerchief on the floor by the couch. She was really rubbing it in, that bitch." Ginny's voice rose to a shriller tone. "Was she good, Tommy?"

"Now, look—"

"Was she better than I've been? I don't see how that could be. She isn't capable of giving everything. Not the way I—No!" Her voice caught and broke and she angrily brushed the back of a hand across her eyes. "It's all right, Tommy. Like I said, I've been watching this coming. You're getting back on your feet. After tonight you won't be just a fisherman. And if the season's any good, which Matt thinks it will be, you'll clean up. Then you'll go on from there. You have what it takes to go on from there. I know that and so does Gail. You can be an important man in this town. You'll be looking back on this little period with me as a kind of nice vacation." Then she snapped, "But has it really been fun?"

"If you'll listen—"

"Have I been amusing?"

"Not that, Ginny, no."

"But a low-class cocktail waitress, a tramp—"

I grabbed her shoulders in my hands and shook her, "Ginny!"

"I shouldn't have said that. Should I? I know better than that. You aren't that way. I'm sorry I said it. I'm spoiling everything. But I am right about tonight. Aren't I?"

"Please. Ginny."

"I know. It's all right, Tommy. For a little while, anyway, our worlds apart came together and it was pretty wonderful, even though I knew it couldn't last." She put her arms about my neck, unmindful of the people on the street. "Shall we say good-by here?" She pressed against me and kissed me hard and then was out of my arms and disappeared through the entrance and into the hotel.

I could still feel her warmth in my arms and took a step toward the hotel, but came to a reluctant halt and turned away to walk slowly down the street.

When I reached the wharf that evening it was swarming with fishermen, all excited by the rumor that the fleet could put to sea in less than an hour. I talked with some of the men and learned that fishing contracts had not yet been signed, but that a number of canners had agreed orally to the forty-dollar price. Moore was one of the last holding out.

Tony rowed up to the wharf with our dory just as the news swept through the crowd of men that, though contracts still had not been signed, all of the canners had agreed to the price and that fishing could be done that night. Crews tumbled into broad-bottomed skiffs about the wharf, yelling and shouting happily at each other, and hauled off for their boats anchored in the harbor. Then the boat owners began arriving from the conference and hurried off in their dories. They expected another bad season, they were none too pleased to be without contracts, but it was obviously a relief to them to be doing something. They all had a prayer on their lips that maybe this season might fool them.

Matt was one of the last to arrive. He came strolling down the wharf with a leather jacket slung over his shoulder and swerved in my direction when he saw me. Gail and Steve Moore were not far behind them. They stopped about ten feet away when Matt faced me with his big feet spread wide apart and his chest looking like an oak cask. My relief at sight of him faded quickly. There was something about the tightness of his expression and the cold, blue steel in his eyes that warned me that something had gone wrong. Gail, too, was watching us rather oddly, like a small child staring with fascination at the burning fuse of a package of firecrackers. Whatever was wrong, she knew all about it, perhaps, I thought, had even inspired it. I remembered how Matt had walked out of the cottage the night before and felt a cold chill of apprehension.

I looked away from Gail and into Matt's eyes. "We'd better get moving. The crew is on hand and the boat's ready for sea."

Matt's lips thinned to a white line as he shook his head. "I'm not going on the *Rosita* with you, Tom."

I gave him a silly smile and said, "What was that again?"

"I'm not going with you. I've had a better offer."

"Hey, wait a minute. I don't get this." I glanced at Gail, but she half closed her eyes and turned away. "What are you talking about?"

"Simple economics, that's all. I've just sold out my partnership. Moore gave me a better deal. He owns a bigger seiner, the *Sea Otter*. So I've traded my interest in the *Rosita* for a sixty per cent cut of the *Sea Otter*. That's all. You're on your own."

I realized he was serious and shouted, "But you can't pull a stunt like that. You can't walk out on me. What the hell do I know about sardines?"

Matt shrugged his powerful shoulders with indifference, but there was a gleam in his eyes that told me he was enjoying the situation I was in. He may as well have said aloud that he had warned me about Gail and that now he was going to make me sweat. "Sorry," he said. "Can't be helped. I've told you before that when I get a better deal I take it. That's all there is to it."

"Why, you lousy, no good—"

I blew my top, stepped in close and slugged him flush on the point of the chin. It was like hitting rock. He was so surprised that I was able to swing again and opened a gash on his cheek with a hard right, but that was as far as I got right then. He swung a huge fist into the pit of my stomach, with all the solid muscle of his body behind it, and I went down. The wharf spun and whirled before my eyes at least a minute before it settled down. I looked up at Matt standing over me, his feet spread wide apart. I glanced at Gail, who was biting her lip, then at Moore, who was laughing. A crowd was beginning to collect around us. Then I looked back at Matt and saw red.

He had thrown his jacket aside and was standing there half-crouched, the battering rams of his fists cocked at his hips, hard lights of wild danger flickering in his eyes. I warmed to that danger and felt a wave of relief sweep through me. It was going to be good. It had to be good, as long as I could make it last.

I got slowly to my feet partly turned away from Matt, then, as quickly as I could, caught him squarely in the mouth with a looping left and felt the pleasant shock of it travel up my arm. He roared like a bull and then we were really at it. He was too big for me and much too strong, but he was also a lot heavier and slower moving. I was considerably faster, however, and in excellent shape, besides having a better knowledge of boxing. I had to box with him, keep away and feint and jab. Whenever I got close the sledge hammers of his fists felt as if they were crushing me. Every time I was hit I thought I would surely go down. But I stayed on my feet and slashed at his face and, losing or not, handed out as much punishment as possible.

The crowd grunted sympathetically each time I was staggered and I could almost feel them praying for me to stay on my feet. Matt had no real defense. He simply kept swinging his big fists in my general direction, knowing that sooner or later he would connect with one that no man could stand against. I had his face soon looking like a busted tomato and, for one wild moment, was even foolish enough to think I could do more to him. I stepped in close, caught him in the stomach with a hard left to bring down his guard, then swung my right for the point of his chin. It was a mistake. Matt's stomach was too hard, his guard did not go down and my right skidded off his forearm. I was trapped in too close, momentarily off balance and helpless. His left crashed into the side of my head and I was slammed back against the side of a warehouse. I tasted blood in my mouth and could not see, but I knew that right was coming. Fortunately for the bones of my jaw, he did not catch me quite flush on the chin, but rather to the side. It was enough, however. I skidded down the wall of the warehouse, pitched on my face and rolled over. I was not exactly unconscious, but neither was I able to move. The fight was all over.

I blinked up at the stars and the crowd and Matt standing looking down at me, his big chest rising and falling with his heavy breathing. Then I noticed something peculiar. The crowd of fishermen, his friends, the men who always had a hearty greeting for him, were scowling and glaring at him. They were not happy with the manner in which our partnership had come to an end. Matt noticed it, too, while wiping the blood from his face with the back of his sleeve. He growled something under his breath, picked up his jacket and rammed his way out through the crowd with his elbows.

I got to my hands and knees, then shakily to my

feet. Moore was grinning at me broadly, as I got out a handkerchief and wiped the blood from my face. He laughed and said genially, "You pick on the wrong men. Better stay in your own league, partner."

I caught the emphasis on the last word and asked, "What was that last?"

He smiled around his cigar and answered, "Why, just partner, that's all."

"Oh, no."

"Yeah," he chuckled, "that's it. Funny, ain't it? You heard Matt tell you he sold out to me. Okay. Figure it out. I'm your new partner."

That was even worse than the beating I had taken. I felt humiliated and defeated and trapped. Moore's statement that I was operating in the wrong league seemed all too true.

He understood how I was feeling. "This," he sneered, "is where we separate the men from the boys. You can step down any time. I'll take care of the *Rosita*."

I looked toward Gail, who was shaking her head at me. Then I understood and told Moore, "You're in the wrong league, you jerk. The major portion of the boat is in my name. You don't even own a full partnership until you pick up the options."

"You forget I hold a note on that scow for eleven thousand."

"Throw that in and it still doesn't make half of the investment involved. You can try a little stepping down yourself. I'm going fishing."

I beckoned to Tony and started along the wharf toward the dory. Tony made no move to go with me. He was looking back at Moore, a question in his eyes.

Moore gave him an almost imperceptible nod, so Tony turned around to join me. We left the lights of the wharf and dropped down to the dory bobbing on the black water below. Tony picked up the oars and started rowing across the harbor toward the *Rosita*. I sat in the bow and looked back at the wharf and saw Gail standing in a pool of light staring after us. She lifted an arm and waved. I shook my head. Nothing was answered. Nothing.

CHAPTER FIFTEEN

The moment we boarded the *Rosita* I was completely lost. What I knew about purse seining was virtually nothing. I had gone with the crew a week before while they made practice sets, but that had served only to confuse me. It took long familiarity to understand the working of that complicated net and years of experience to know where to place it. I knew nothing. But I was still compelled to go fishing regardless of results.

At least, I knew how to run the boat. The diesel engine was already turning over, the running lights were on and the crew was aboard. I went into the galley, where one of the men delegated as cook was preparing a *ciappino* dinner, washed the blood from my face, pasted adhesive over a gash on my chin, then went up to the dark bridge. Pete and Johnson were waiting for me. Their eyes were silently asking questions, but I hadn't the answers. As soon as a man below threw off the buoy line I nodded at Pete to let out the clutch and we were underway. Where we were going I didn't know, but we were moving and that, for the moment, was the big thing as far as I was concerned.

It was a bright night, the heavens covered with a full panoply of stars. I enjoyed that, but Pete and Johnson were glum. Light made it difficult to find the schools of sardines. Their milky trace in the water could be confused with the light of stars. I doubted if we would find sardines, anyway, so paid little attention. The night felt good to me. I had the wheel and followed the bobbing lights of the long line of purse seiners ahead of us, all heading across the bay in the general direction of Santa Cruz. I assumed they knew where they were going, so there was no other course but to follow.

Pete and Johnson went below when dinner was served, but I remained on the bridge and watched the shore lights of Fort Ord, Capitola, Watsonville and other towns like thin ribbons on the eastern horizon. I was trying not to think and doing it successfully. But when Pete, Tony, Johnson and other members of the crew came up on the bridge I had to face them. Their livelihood, after all, was dependent on getting fish. They were not interested in my problems.

I looked them all over, then turned to Johnson. "How long have you been after sardines?"

He shrugged. "A long time. Fifteen—twenty years, I guess."

"And Pete?"

"Longer. He broke me in."

"Okay, Pete. I suppose you know how to find sardines

and net them?"

Pete grinned. "Been doing it all my life."

"Good. Then you're in command. Understand? I'll run the boat, but you run the fishing and we all take orders from you. Can you do it that way?"

He glanced around at the other men, a worried frown of sudden responsibility creasing his brows, then his smile returned. "We'll get fish."

Tony shouted against the wind, "Hey, wait a minute. This ain't no way to get sardines. We need a proper skipper—"

"If you don't like it," I said, "you can get the hell off the bridge and stay in the galley."

"Yeah? Who's gonna—"

"I am. Get moving or shut up."

Tony stood facing me squarely for a moment only. He turned away and leaned against the bridge railing, swearing under his breath. Another cheap victory, but nevertheless it felt good.

Pete told everyone to go below and disappeared for a few minutes himself to listen to the fleet reports coming in over the radio. When he came back to the bridge he reported excitedly that some of the boats in the middle of the bay were already on sardines and that the schools looked big, as Matt had predicted. Then he switched on the fathometer by the wheel and the two of us watched the small red lights indicating, on the left, zero surface and, on the right, depth in fathoms. A third red light flashed on and off for a few seconds between them. Pete explained, "Just passed over a small school." So that was the way it worked.

Within the next few hours, while cruising back and

forth between Santa Cruz and Capitola, we passed over many small schools. I began learning how to identify their milky shape in the water ahead of us and anticipated Pete's commands to swing the boat over them to estimate the size of the school. He remained dissatisfied with their size until two in the morning.

We were swinging around another big seiner that was already hauling in its net when the third light on the fathometer began blinking and suddenly merged into the other two lights. Pete whispered, "Jee-zuss, this is it. A big one. Circle to port and I'll figure the direction they're heading." I swung to port and completed a circle and Pete had me keep the bow swinging. The head of the school was at the other end of the arc.

Pete reached over to clang the bridge bell and the whole crew spilled out on the aft deck. A man jumped into the enormously broad skiff and the others stood by ready to heave it off. Pete yelled at them and the skiff plopped off of the stern into the black water. It tugged along at the end of a linc while the men took their positions about the great mound of the piled net, then Pete yelled another direction. The skiff fell astern, line paid out and then the net began pouring into the sea. I continued circling to port, meanwhile, then saw the skiff coming up ahead of me and slowed down. In another moment we were dead in the water, and the circle of the net was complete.

Pete ran below and I followed after him. As soon as the net's bowline was made secure to the port bow of the boat the skiff man began hauling in net. The men aboard also hauled in lines, then had the steel cables singing around the power winches. The big net was slowly drawn in at the top and closed by cable at the bottom somewhat in the way a purse is closed. The sardines were trapped between the net and an underwater light blinking on and off under the hull of the boat. When the gap of the two ends closed the school of fish was secured. Johnson estimated the size of the school at close to a hundred tons.

An hour later the men were still closing the net and pulling some of it aboard the boat. They were pulling the net in such a fashion that the whole school would finally be concentrated in a relatively small pocket directly against the port side of the boat. I helped as much as I could.

We were making excellent progress when the skiff man shouted at the top of his lungs, "My God, the bowline's gone!" The whole crew froze. I looked up along the deck of the boat just as the end of the bowline slithered over the bulwarks and into the sea. I knew nothing of purse seining, but anyone could understand what was going to happen next. The end of the net would spill open and the whole school of fish would be lost. The night's fishing would be over.

I was the only one aboard not wearing sea boots and unencumbered by slickers and oilskin trousers. For the first time, in a situation of danger, I acted not with an urge to meet the danger as something desirable, but for an entirely different reason. I could not allow the men to see their whole night's work go unrewarded and return to port empty-handed. I ripped off the leather jacket, ran forward along the deck and dived overboard. I landed in a sea boiling with sardines, but when I came up I saw the rope. It was going down fast. I grabbed the end of the line and was almost pulled under with it, but also managed to grab an end of the net. My arms felt as if they were being pulled out of their sockets and I knew what it was like to be placed on a rack. I hung on and got my head above water and grabbed higher up the net, inching my fingers along, then two of the crewmen took the line from me and hurried forward to again secure it on the bow. Johnson reached down and lifted me from the water to the deck, where I was suddenly so weak I could hardly stand.

His eyes were like ice as he growled, "I fastened that line myself. It don't just come loose all alone."

I sucked in huge lungfuls of air, then asked, "Have we lost the school?"

"No. Maybe half. Fifty tons is a damn fine haul. Don't you worry. We get 'em in."

I glanced over at Tony who was helping at one of the winches and doubted that he had been there when the line went overboard. But there was no time to investigate anything. The important thing was closing the rest of the net and getting the fish aboard. There was not even time for me to change clothes. I went back to work still soaking wet.

We were drifting close to the other big seiner by that time. When its stern swung by us I read the name SEA OTTER. I looked up on the bridge and there was Matt's giant figure leaning on the rail. He raised his hand toward me in a half-hearted wave and I opened my mouth to swear at him, but started grinning instead. He had known exactly what he was doing in leaving me flat and had probably figured that I would be seriously crippled by his action. But I wondered if, in his boots, I would not have done the same thing. Taking sixty per cent of the *Sea Otter* was certainly a more sensible deal than stringing along with an amateur partner. Furthermore, it placed him many steps closer to his goal. I could hardly blame him for not deviating from his single-minded purpose, even though the odds seemed stacked against him. Besides, we were getting fish without his help and that made me feel even better.

When he moved away to look in another direction, back toward Monterey, I turned to peer around the bow of our boat. I saw lights coming toward us fast, then heard the purr of a high-speed engine. In another moment a speedboat came into sight and slowed down in the water close by the *Sea Otter*. I could hear something being yelled to Matt, but could not make out the words. Matt turned and pointed in our direction. The speedboat backed away, swung about and crossed the narrow expanse of water to the starboard side of the *Rosita*. It was flooded in the dozens of lights on our masts as it swung alongside and cut its motor.

Gail was seated in the stern cockpit of the boat. Moore was standing at her side, looking up at us, grinning again. But also in the stern cockpit was a lean-looking individual who spelled LAW in capital letters.

The latter cupped his hands about his mouth and called, "Tom Howie?"

I stepped to the railing and looked down at him. "I'm Howie."

"Then you're the man I want. I'm deputy-sheriff Callahan. You've taken a boat to sea without the owner's permission."

"You've been listening to the wrong people, officer. I happen to be the owner."

Callahan shrugged. "That means nothing to me. You can argue that out with someone else. I got a warrant for you."

He reached up and grabbed at the railing. I lifted a fist and smashed it down on his fingers. He let go and dropped back into the speedboat to stare at me in open-mouthed amazement.

I asked him, "Do you also happen to be a U. S. Marshal and a member of the Coast Guard?" When he shook his head I said, "I didn't think so. You have to be one or the other or both to board a ship at sea. Come aboard this boat and I'll have you tied up in the engine room. Try to use force and I'll blow your brains out and be legally justified."

Moore had lost his grin and screamed, "He's bluffing. He can't do nothing to you. Goddamn it, man, you represent the law."

Callahan ruefully examined his fingers and shook his head. "He's right, Mr. Moore."

"Serve that warrant on him."

Callahan sighed. "Sorry, Mr. Moore. Can't be done. I told you before this is just a bluff on your part. He knows marine law." He dropped back to his seat and wrapped a handkerchief around his crushed fingers.

Moore turned away from him to yell up at the crew,

"Listen to me, all of you. I own half of this outfit and I say I don't want fish brought in tonight. Understand? All of you know who I am. You follow the orders of this phony and I'll personally blackball every one of you. You got that?"

The crew looked over the port side at the net teeming with sardines. Fifty tons represented two thousand dollars. The cut of each of them would be over a hundred dollars for one night's work. It was money in the pocket and the season promised to be good. They were on a boat and they were working. Simple thinking, but it added up. They looked back at Moore and started to laugh. They were going my way.

Moore sagged back in his seat like a sack of potatoes. He leaned forward to tap the shoulder of the man at the wheel and waved his hand to pull away.

Gail stood up and stared at Moore, then looked up at me with a smile. "Have you any objections about my coming aboard?"

I looked down and saw her working the gaudy diamond ring from her finger. She got it loose and dropped it into Moore's lap. I don't think he was especially surprised, though he did make a move to grab her arm, but then dropped his hand in defeat. Gail's eyes came back to mine and she raised her hands toward me. I leaned over the rail, grabbed her under the arms and swung her aboard. She stood at my side, searching my eyes, as I watched the speedboat pull away and head toward the *Sea Otter*.

There was no time to talk with her. The men now had the net closed in a tight pocket and my hands were needed to help. Gail went above and disappeared in the bridge cabin as I went back to work. When she came out on the bridge a few minutes later she was wearing a pair of my old slacks, sea boots and a woolen shirt much too big for her. Her hair was loose about her shoulders and flying in the wind and the lights of the boat were sparkling in her eyes. It was beautiful and I was properly entranced, but I had to work.

The brailing net with its long pole was swung over the side by the boom and dipped into the mass of fish. The winch screamed, the hoop of the net came up and was fastened over the open hold and then the tail of the net came up and sardines spilled through the hatch like a silver flood. It took us better than an hour to brail all the fish from the main net and into the hold. When the operation was through we had about fifty-four tons. The men secured the rest of the net and started cleaning up on deck. They were tired, but they were happy. The future was no longer bleak. The fish were back and they were safe.

I went into the galley for two cups of coffee and came out to hear a loud splash. I looked overboard and saw Tony swimming toward the *Sea Otter*. All of his fishing clothes had also been thrown in the water. Pete and Johnson were standing at the railing watching him with smugly satisfied smiles.

Pete laughed and winked at me. "You ain't in this, skipper. We done it."

"Was he the one who let the bowline loose?"

"Yeah. Swede, here, caught him trying to set fire to the engine room. Swede kind of roughed him up a little, I believe."

Johnson grunted, "Uh-huh. Bad egg, that Tony. I

guess maybe he's on Moore's payroll. Now he can work at it."

The two of them burst into loud, raucous laughter and slapped each other on the back.

I went up to the bridge, handed a cup of coffee to Gail, then let out the engine clutch and turned the throttle. We began to move. I swung the boat about and headed toward Monterey. Off to our left, over the mountains, was the first hint of dawn. I felt as clean and washed as the lightening of the sky. I had done nothing big, or great, or anything to boast about, yet I felt as if a miracle had been accomplished and I was proud of it. Whipping Moore and getting sardines aboard were not so important. The most heart-warming thing had been the attitude of the crew. They had included me as one of themselves, they had accepted my weak leadership and they had chosen to stand by me rather than Moore. It made me feel very pleased and also a little humble.

Standing there, suddenly thinking about it, I also became aware of the fact that the death wish had disappeared somewhere along the line. There was no longer an impelling urge to court danger, to deliberately place myself in a position or to cause a situation in which death could be the end result. That wild burden was gone and I felt a constriction in my throat as I realized who was responsible for the cure.

I turned to look at Gail, standing by the wheel and facing into the wind. I said, "That was quite a gamble, Gail."

Her eyes came about and she was smiling at me. "What was, Tom?"

"Dropping that ring in Moore's lap. That was probably the biggest gamble you ever made in your life. It took more courage than most people will ever know. It isn't easy to throw away an absolute certainty for a question mark."

"I don't care." She tucked a hand under my arm and placed a cheek against my shoulder. "I had to do it. It wasn't something I thought out. It just had to be done as soon as possible."

"Of course. Sooner or later, it had to be done, though probably for other reasons."

She looked up at me with a puzzled expression. "I don't understand. What other reasons are you talking about? I did it for one reason—you."

"Well, we'll talk about that later. Right now," I said, "I'm hungry as hell. How about bringing some breakfast up to the bridge?"

We made the run into Monterey in about two hours and a half and warped up to a buoy near the Holbrook and Stevens hopper. Another seiner was unloading and we had to stand by to wait our turn. Gail went into the bridge cabin and changed back to the clothes she had been wearing before. When she came out she came quickly to my side, where I was leaning over the spray shield, and linked an arm through mine.

The time was right and at last I thought I knew the answers.

I turned to look into the smile in Gail's eyes and asked her, "Did you drop that ring in Moore's lap for the sake of Tom Howie, a fisherman?"

She frowned at me. "How do you mean?"

"I mean that you aren't interested in me as a

fisherman."

"Well, no, of course not." She was smiling again as she said, "I have a strong hunch about you. This boat won't satisfy you very long. You'll use it for a while, until you get farther ahead, then you'll go on to bigger things. There is a drive in you that will force you on."

"And you're counting on it. But suppose I'm satisfied with the way things are?"

"Oh, no," she laughed. "Impossible. I've been watching you too long. You see, my darling, I think I know how you are. You know what better living is like, you've experienced it, but somehow you lost it. Now you are on your way back. And you'll go farther than anyone I know."

"Including Moore?"

"Far beyond Steve. He doesn't have your capabilities."

"So you've made up your mind to hitch your little wagon to what looks like a star."

She squeezed my arm and laughed at me. "Is anything wrong with that?"

"I'm sorry, Gail, but there is. I have lived what you think is a better life. I don't want it again. I don't ever want it again." I waved an arm to embrace the boats and the sea and the horizon. "I like this. I like it beyond anything I have ever had. For the first time in my life I've found myself."

"But you can't be serious. You'll never be satisfied with just fishing."

"I am already more than satisfied with it. I wouldn't trade it for all the oil wells in California."

"Oh, no!"

"I'm afraid that's the way it is. All I am interested in now is in paying off Moore and continuing fishing and learning and in the future, if it can be done, I'd like to be known as the good skipper of a good boat. That is my goal."

Her eyes went wide and she gripped my arms hard, her fingers biting in like talons. "You're out of your mind. You can't do it that way. Tom, I've taken a wild gamble on you."

"You had to take that gamble, but not necessarily for me. You aren't for me any more than you are for Moore. He seemed to be the man, for a while, but you couldn't go through with it. You used any excuse to get out of it. I looked like a good one. But I am not the man, either. You can't seem to get it through your head yet, but one day you will. You belong to a man who is more of a man than Moore and I put together."

"No," she screamed. Her arms went about me and she held tightly, her head against my chest. "Please, Tom. It isn't Matt. I won't be married to a fisherman. I won't. I can't."

"But I'm a fisherman, too, and I intend staying that way. I mean it, Gail. Matt, though, has other ideas. He won't remain simply a fisherman for very long. I know his ambitions. All he wants right now is to get on his feet. It looks as if this season will do it. Then ask him to take over your cannery and see what he says."

She had started to sob, but that came to an abrupt halt. I could almost feel the wheels spinning in her mind. Slowly the grip of her arms relaxed and she leaned back to frown at me. "Do you think he would do it?"

"I'll gamble this boat on it. Now, frankly, of the three of us, who do you think is the better equipped to run your cannery, get it out of the red and restore your fortunes?" While she was thinking that over, I looked over her shoulder and saw the *Sea Otter* coming in to a hopper farther up the line. I pointed it out to her and said, "Get one of the crew to row you over. I'll see the two of you later on."

She turned away from me to stare thoughtfully toward the *Sea Otter* and I knew there would be no more argument.

The seiner in front of us had moved away, so I swung the *Rosita* away from the buoy and alongside the hopper. The crew immediately started unloading sardines from the hold and into the square hopper, where they were sucked down through big pipes under water and into the cannery. The process would take a couple of hours, but I had to get ashore.

I went below, pushed the dory into the water and asked Pete to row me to shore. As we pulled away I looked up at the slim figure standing on the bridge. She waved to me once, but her attention again returned to the *Sea Otter* and to the giant figure of a man on its bridge.

As soon as we reached the cannery I jumped impatiently up to the wooden landing and waved Pete away. I walked up the landing and around to the front of the cannery and to a store across the street, where I telephoned for a taxi. As soon as it arrived I went into Monterey, got out on the main street and headed for a jewelry shop. When I mentioned engagement rings, the clerk appraised the working clothes I was wearing, sniffed audibly and placed a tray of cheap rings on the counter. I selected one with a diamond so small it could hardly be seen. It was exactly what I wanted. Anything else would have been crude.

I was about to call the Martinelli residence, but had a hunch that I would draw a blank. I hurried down Alvarado Street, crossed the tracks to the wharf and started out between the lines of shops and sea-food restaurants.

Ginny was standing at the far end of the wharf, her black hair gleaming in the sun and blowing loosely in the light breeze. It was natural for her to be there. It was her heritage to watch the fleet leave the hoppers and return to harbor. She was watching them come in one by one, but she was also looking beyond at the long line of seiners still at the hoppers. The *Rosita*, at that distance, looked like any of the other seiners disgorging their fat, but I had no doubt she could distinguish it and had her eyes fastened on it. She was there where she belonged, waiting, even though she had said good-by. That, too, was her heritage.

I hurried toward her, at last having found everything I was seeking and knowing all the answers to all the questions that every man has to ask some time in his life. In another moment I would have her in my arms and there would never again be another question to ask.

I noticed the police car parked at the edge of the wharf, but it meant nothing to me. I saw the little man in the shiny blue serge suit leaning against the car and still it meant nothing. Every cell of my body was rushing to meet Ginny. I was really conscious of nothing else until the little man in the blue serge suit grabbed my arm and it was Kinnan, the investigator from Los Angeles.

Even now, now that I have had time to think about it, I don't know how I felt at that moment. When Kinnan said, "Hello, Mr. Carleton," there was numbness and shock, of course, a feeling of being suddenly drained empty. But there was more to it than that, of thoughts of Ginny and of Bunny lying before the fireplace and a gun that was not meant to be used. Especially the gun. It loomed in my mind's eye the size of a cannon.

It was probably some time before I was able to say anything and then my voice was a hoarse croak: "How did you know?"

He looked apologetic and even embarrassed as he said, "It was something you said about the gun last time I saw you. It kept going around and around in my head for weeks and weeks. Then I had an idea what it was that was bothering me and looked into it and found out I was right."

I glanced at the two policemen, who had not left the squad car, but were watching us with interest, then back at Kinnan. "Something I said?"

"Yeah. The only way you, I mean you as a fisherman, would know anything about that Holt shooting would be from what you read in the papers. You made a crack about Carleton leaving that gun in her apartment. Remember?"

"Yes."

"That was right. But when you made the crack you

said that it was a borrowed gun. That was right, too. Only one thing wrong with it. That little piece of information about the gun being borrowed was never in the papers."

I sucked in a deep breath of air and blew it out slowly. "So you've come to take me back?"

He dropped his hand from my arm and squinted at me curiously. "Are you suffering from amnesia, Mr. Carleton?"

"Not at all."

"You remember everything?"

"Mostly. I was pretty drunk that night. There are a few blank spots."

He shook his head, a deep puzzle in his eyes. "I don't get it. I've been thinking about it for a long time now, ever since I knew you were Carleton, and I still don't get it." He waved his hand to indicate the squad car and said, "That's why I brought these cops along, for my own protection. I thought maybe you'd be violent, or a little cracked, or something."

I said wearily, "I'm all right."

"Yeah. Maybe. You know, only one idea even begins to make sense to me. So tell me something? How many Los Angeles newspapers have you read since that night?"

I thought of it and answered, "Two. An early edition that following morning and another one about three or four days later."

"None in between and none since?"

"No."

"Okay." He nodded his head slowly, resolving something in his mind. "I guess that's it," he said. "So tell me something else. Why are you hiding out this way?"

I glanced at Ginny, who was still looking out over the harbor, and replied, "Isn't that obvious? I have no more desire to face a murder rap than the next man. It was an accident, it must have happened when I passed out, but who would believe me?"

He stared at me and said softly, "Jee-zuss, what a thing to live with! I really feel for you. Look, Mr. Carleton; the cops picked up that dame's husband a few hours after the first papers were out and he broke and confessed the whole thing."

I turned slowly to stare at him and reached out to grab his arms in my hands, shaking him slowly back and forth. "What in God's name are you talking about?"

"It was the Holt guy who did it. That's what I'm telling you. That gun you left wasn't the murder gun. The cops thought so, at first, then found out it hadn't been fired. Besides, the slug that killed her was from a thirty-two. They'd already seen this Holt and remembered how nervous he'd been. So they talked with him again and he broke down."

"Good God! Nicky!"

"Yeah. The way I got it from the cops, this Holt said he'd seen your car in front of his wife's place and went up to the apartment. The door was unlocked. He went in and saw his wife standing in front of the fireplace and you in a chair."

"That draught on the back of my neck. That's when I passed out."

"I guess. Anyway, he wanted to kill somebody, the

two of you, maybe. So he shot his wife. But when it came to shooting you he lost his nerve and scrammed. That's the way it happened. And all this time you've been thinking—"

It was a good thing I was holding to his arms or I would have fallen. A wave of nausea swept through me and for a moment I thought I would be sick, but it passed. I squeezed Kinnan's shoulders and patted his back and grinned like a fool and all I could think of saying was, "You stay here. Stay right here."

I left him and walked down the wharf to Ginny. She turned and stared at me and saw my expression and there were stars in her eyes, even though for a few moments she must have thought I was drunk. But when I took the little ring from my pocket her eyes brimmed with tears and she had to bite her lip to hold them back. I put an arm about her waist and looked out over the harbor and the purse seiners streaming in and down the long row of canneries and over the broad horizons of the sea and felt what a good thing it was just to be alive. Now with a new thing to do and a new life to live I would no longer be isolated on a mountain top. I could walk among men as one of them and Ginny, always at my side, would lead me through the valleys.

It was good.

THE END

H. VERNOR DIXON BIBLIOGRAPHY
(1908-1984)

NOVELS
Laughing Gods (1935)
Something for Nothing (1950)
To Hell Together (1951; abridged edition, 1959)
Deep is the Pit (1952)
The Marriage Bed (1952)
Too Rich to Die (1953)
Up a Winding Stair (1953)
A Lover for Cindy (1954)
The Hunger and the Hate (1955)
Cry Blood (1956)
Killer in Silk (1956)
That Girl Marian (1962)
Guerrilla (1963)
The Pleasure Seekers (1963)
The Rag Pickers (1966)
The Moon is Green (unpublished)

STORIES
The Experimenter (*Collier's*, July 25 1936)
Not in the Book (*Collier's*, Sept 26 1936)
Experience Not Necessary (*Collier's*, Aug 7 1937)
Tennis Bum (*The American Magazine*, Feb 1939)
The Captains Bride (*The American Magazine*, Mar 1939)
One Was Enough (*The American Magazine*, Aug 1939)
Clear and Unlimited (*Collier's*, Aug 12 1939)
Inquire of the Sea (*The American Magazine*, Sept 1939)
Poodle on a Leash (*The American Magazine*, Nov 1939)
Bali Love Song (*The American Magazine,* Apr 1940)
The Sharks of Hihimanu (*Cosmopolitan*, June 1940)

The Siren Smiled (*The American Magazine*, July, Aug, Sept, Oct, Nov 1940)

Manhattan Jungle (*The American Magazine*, Mar 1941)

Generals Make Promises (*The American Magazine*, May 1941; *Argosy* (UK), Feb 1942)

Call Me Edie, Honey! (*The American Magazine*, Aug 1941)

Test Flight (*Cosmopolitan*, July 1942)

Women Like a Beating (*The American Magazine*, July 1942)

The Game Is for Mary (*The American Magazine*, Sept 1942)

Built for a Pilot (*Collier's*, Dec 12 1942)

Civilian Pilot (*Collier's*, Jan 30 1943)

Follow the Leader (*Collier's*, Mar 6 1943)

Flat-Top Jenny (*Cosmopolitan*, Oct 1943)

The Eager Beaver (*Collier's*, Dec 11 1943)

Only Bats Fly Blind (*Argosy*, Jan 1944)

Via the Horn and Hell (*Argosy*, Feb 1944)

Harpooner's Lady (*Argosy*, Mar 1944)

There Was a Girl— (*The American Magazine*, Apr 1944)

A Guy Like Red (*Collier's*, Apr 15 1944)

Come in Like a Yankee! (*Argosy*, June 1944)

No Imagination (*Liberty*, July 1 1944)

Grandstand Flyer (*Argosy*, Sept 1944)

The Better Things (*Liberty*, Sept 9 1944)

How to Fight a War (*Argosy*, Oct 1944)

The Bobby-Sock Bride (*Liberty*, Nov 11 1944)

A Dog of Character (*Argosy*, Feb 1945; *Argosy* (Canada), Nov 1945)

Navigator to Colonel (*Argosy*, Mar 1945)

'Round the Horn to Hell (*Argosy*, Apr 1945)

Overnight Diver (*Argosy*, May 1945)

A Downright Peaceful Man! (*Argosy*, June 1945)

The Go-Devil (*The Blue Book Magazine*, July 1945)

You Can't Win (*Cosmopolitan*, Sept 1945)

To Act As God (*Liberty*, Dec 22 1945)

Moonlight (*Cosmopolitan*, Jan 1946)

Is This to Be Our Tomorrow? (*The Blue Book Magazine*, Apr 1946)

The Cub (*Collier's*, Apr 27 1946)

The Black-Haired Widow (*Liberty*, May 25 1946)

The Little Woman (*Liberty*, Aug 17 1946)

The Artist and the Heiress (*The American Magazine*, Mar 1947)

The Pitch to Rio (*The Saturday Evening Post*, Sept 6 1947)

100 Fathoms (*Liberty*, May 1949)

Deep Salvage (*Liberty*, Dec 1949, Jan, Feb, Mar 1950)

Trapped! (*This Week*, 1950; *Suspense* (UK), Apr 1960)

This Is Jo— (*Argosy*, Jan 1950)

The Reef (*Argosy* (UK), May 1950)

Murder Flies High (*The American Magazine*, July 1956)

The Bartender Bit (*Cosmopolitan*, Nov 1957)

STORY COLLECTION

Come in Like a Yankee and Other Stories (1944)

Harry Vernor Dixon was born in 1908 in Sacramento, California. After attending the California School of Fine Arts in San Francisco, he went into show business as an eccentric dancer, headlining with R.K.O., Paramount-Publix and the Orpheum. Dixon published his first novel, the Jazz Age

Laughing Gods, in 1935, then went on to write a number of popular short stories for magazines like *Saturday Evening Post, Cosmopolitan, Atlantic Weekly*, etc., until returning to the novel form in 1950 with *Something for Nothing*. Most of his novels featured a social-climbing outsider, dealing more with the consequences of character than crime. Dixon eventually settled in the Monterey area with his wife, son and daughter—an area where he set most of his novels—entertaining his friends at parties with his rich voice and endless stories. Dixon passed away in 1984.